BY JUSTIN RICHARDS

SIMON AND SCHUSTER

Acknowledgements

*As ever I am indebted to my family – Alison, Julian
and Christian – for their patience, comments
and love, and to my editor, Stephen Cole,
for his comments, patience and confidence.*

SIMON AND SCHUSTER

First published in Great Britain by Simon & Schuster UK Ltd, 2005
A Viacom company

1 3 5 7 9 10 8 6 4 2

Simon & Schuster UK Ltd
Africa House
64-78 Kingsway
London WC2B 6AH

A CIP catalogue record for this book is available from the British Library

ISBN 1 416 90107 8

Typeset by SX Composing DTP, Rayleigh, Essex
Printed and bound in Great Britain by Cox & Wyman, Reading, Berkshire

*For Toby and Jane, neither of whom
suffer from Stage Fright*

CHAPTER ONE

It was a voice that came from everywhere and nowhere. The words were indistinct, on the very edge of understanding.

At first, Mary Foster thought it was her mother calling from the upper gallery. She could not make out the words, but the tone was urgent and determined. She called back, putting down her brush and hurrying across the stage to the auditorium of the theatre. But as she jumped down from the stage, the voice seemed to fade and whisper away to nothing.

'Mum? Mum, is that you?'

Mary's own voice was nervous and shrill. It sounded small and lost in the vast space. There was no answer.

Mary listened for a moment longer. Still there was no reply. Her mother must have finished in the gallery and was probably cleaning the foyer by now. What Mary had heard must have been the traffic outside the theatre. An omnibus in the road outside perhaps. Or the wind. Or . . . She returned to the backstage area and retrieved her brush. She had been sweeping the corridor past the dressing rooms.

The Castle Theatre did not look like a theatre. Remove the stage and the audience seating, and it would be a castle, in fact as well as in name. Even the corridor that Mary was sweeping was like the inside of some medieval fortress. Huge uneven flagstones and rough stone walls made the whole place seem old and claustrophobic. The doors to the dressing rooms and storerooms were thick oak, set into arched frames with large, heavy keys in the locks. The sound of Mary's footsteps, her voice, even the scuff of her brush echoed along the corridor as she cleaned.

She was taking her time, making a good job of it. After all, she had only worked here a fortnight – since leaving school. Now that old Janey Taylor had retired there were just the two of them – Mary and her mum. At this time of night, with the last performance long since ended and the audience, the actors and even the manager, Mr Gregson, gone home over two hours ago, they had the theatre to themselves. By the time they left, dawn would be breaking and they would both be ready for bacon and eggs and a morning sleep.

The brush moved rhythmically across the uneven floor. The bristles seemed to keep time like a song. Sometimes Mary did sing, using the metre of the tune to govern the strokes of the brush. But tonight they seemed to have a rhythm all of their own as she pushed the brush. Push-push-push . . . Push-push-push.

Her arms tiring, Mary paused. But the rhythm continued. Like a tune that she couldn't get out of her mind. The same rhythm, over and over. It was as if she could still hear the swish of the broom across the floor.

'*Scale of dragon, tooth of wolf . . .*'

Mary could almost hear the words of the song in her head.

'*Witches' mummy . . .*'

Just odd snatches. The rest was indistinct.

And she realised with a slow horror that she really could hear the words. It was the voice she had heard before. Whispering like the brush sliding across the floor. A rhythmic chant that seemed to emanate from the walls, the floor, the water pipes that ran along the ceiling – all around.

'*Silvered in the moon's eclipse . . .*'

Mary dropped the brush. The wooden handle clattered to the floor, the sound dead and abrupt as the whispering swirled round her. She ran, her feet slapping on the flagstones. But as she ran, mingled with the sound of her own breath and the slap of her feet, she could still hear the voice. It seemed to follow her down the corridor. It turned with her into the next passage. It kept time with her running towards the steps. She didn't know where she was running, she just had to get away.

Mary had never been down the steps before, never been in the cellar beneath the theatre. She knew that some of the props and scenery were stored there, but it was not her job to clean in the cellar. Even with the lights on, the stone steps at the end of the passage were dim and forbidding – leading down into shadowy blackness.

But with the voice still chasing her, Mary had nowhere else to go. She paused at the top of the stairs, looked over her shoulder along the passageway.

'*Double, double*,' a voice whispered close to her ear.

She gasped at the sound.

'*Toil and trouble . . .*'

Another shriek.

'What do you want?' Mary screamed. 'Who are you?'

She started down the steps. The blackness seemed to beckon her onwards. She stopped again, torn between whether to dare the dark or the voice.

'*Fire burn, and cauldron bubble.*'

Now the voice seemed to come from ahead of her – from the darkness of the cellar. If anything it was louder. A cackle of inhuman laughter echoed round the stairwell. Mary gave a squeal of fear and leaped back up the stairs. To see a dark shadow fall across the end of the corridor. It looked like a woman, only misshapen and twisted. The nose was a jutting beak, the figure was slouched and stunted, broken and bent where the floor met the wall.

Mary found she was unable to move. Even her trembling seemed to have stopped. It was as if time stood still for a moment.

Then a figure followed the shadow into the passageway. And a voice whispered in Mary's ear, '*By the pricking of my thumbs, something wicked this way comes . . .*'

If the voice said anything more, it was lost in the sound of Mary's screams.

'And you are sure the girl's story is to be believed?' the Invisible Detective asked.

His voice was unnaturally loud in the silent room. The usual shuffling and murmuring of his audience seemed to have stopped as Elizabeth Foster told her story. From behind the curtain, Meg could just make out the shadow of the back of the detective's chair. As always, the chair faced away from the audience in the dimly lit room. All they would be able to see of Brandon Lake, the Invisible Detective, was an occasional hand emerging to make a gesture or describe a point. A simple but convincing illusion.

Because, as Meg knew, there was actually no such person as Brandon Lake. The figure in the chair – the owner of the hand that was occasionally seen, the person whose voice now echoed round the room and held his audience spellbound – was really Meg's friend Art Drake. Together with Meg and the other Cannoniers – Jonny and Flinch – Art solved the mysteries and answered the questions that people put to the Invisible Detective at his Monday evening consulting sessions above the locksmith's shop on Cannon Street.

Jonny was standing with Meg behind the curtain in the bay of the window. Like Art and

Meg, he was fourteen years old. He stood as still and silent as Meg, his dark eyes shining as they caught the last of the evening light from outside the dusty window. He was holding a fishing rod, ready to cast a scrawled note secretly across to Art in the chair if they needed to tell him anything.

'Was the girl lying?' Jonny whispered to Meg.

Meg shrugged. 'I don't know without hearing her tell the story,' she admitted. 'But her mother believes it. She's not lying.' If she was, Meg would know at once. She always did.

'She's a good girl, my Mary,' the woman was saying. 'She wouldn't make something like that up. Besides, she was scared out of her wits. Screaming fit to burst when she saw my shadow on the wall as I ran to find her.'

'Distorted by the angle of the light, no doubt,' Art replied, keeping his voice deep as he played the role of Brandon Lake. 'Perhaps that was enough to stimulate her imagination and make her think she was hearing a voice?'

'She was frightened well before she saw me,' Mrs Foster replied. 'She heard something right enough. I . . .' She broke off, as if realising she had said too much.

7

Meg was about to scribble a note to Art, to tell him the woman was keeping something back. But Art knew that already.

'Yes, Mrs Foster?' he prompted. 'You were saying?'

The woman's voice was quieter, less assured as she answered. 'I was just going to say . . . well –' she seemed to gather her confidence as she went on – 'well, it ain't just my Mary. Janey Taylor, she said she heard voices too. Whispering and chanting. All round the theatre. She's old, of course, getting past being able to clean properly. But that wasn't why she left the job. She left because of the voices.' Mrs Foster drew a deep, audible breath. 'That theatre's haunted,' she declared. 'I know it is.'

There was a pause after this claim. Then the Invisible Detective said quietly, 'You've heard the voices too, haven't you, Mrs Foster?'

'Yes,' the woman admitted, her own voice a ghostly whisper in the darkened room. 'Yes, by my soul, I've heard the ghost of the Castle Theatre.'

The session drew to a close shortly after this revelation. The Invisible Detective promised to investigate the strange case of the Castle Theatre, but pointed out, to the amusement of some of his audience, that he was not qualified to perform exorcisms.

But Mrs Foster seemed satisfied with this. If Mr Lake could reassure her that the spirits were not malevolent and meant no harm to them, she could persuade her daughter that there was nothing to worry about.

When the last of the audience had departed noisily down the wooden stairs and into Cannon Street, Meg, Jonny and Flinch emerged from behind the curtains. Jonny drew the curtains back to let the last of the evening light into the dusty room. He went to count the evening's takings – the detective charged sixpence for every question – while Art threw off the enormous coat he wore to complete the illusion that he was Brandon Lake, the Invisible Detective.

Meg went to help him with the coat. Her long auburn hair glowed a fiery red in the dying light. Flinch followed closely behind. She was the youngest of the Cannoniers, being only about nine or ten. She was short and slight of build, with long fair hair that was distinctly bedraggled and stained almost grey with dirt and dust.

To tell the truth, she did not really know exactly how old she was. For as long as Flinch, or any of them, could remember, she had lived out on the streets. She had no family that she knew of apart from Meg, Jonny and Art. The closest she had to a home was the old carpet warehouse that the children had made their den and where Flinch slept, curled up in a nest of old carpet fragments with a couple of thin blankets to keep her warm, and the rats to keep her company. Compared to what she was used to before she met Art and the others, it was luxury.

'Is the Castle Theatre really haunted?' Flinch wanted to know as soon as Art was free of the coat.

'I have no idea,' he confessed, sweeping a lick of dark brown hair away from his forehead. 'To be honest, I wouldn't have thought it was old enough.'

'When was it built?' Meg wanted to know.

'Must be since the war,' Art said. 'I think the furnishings are all old and it's made to look like a castle inside – all stone and statues and suits of armour dotted about the place. But I remember Dad told me once there used to be a workhouse there or something.' He grinned. 'It will be fun investigating its history and finding out,' he decided.

'But is it haunted?' Flinch still wanted to know. 'Are there ghosts?' Her tone was eager but nervous.

Meg sighed. 'There's no such things as ghosts, Flinch,' she said.

'There are!' the younger girl insisted. 'Remember that haunted house on Jursall Street?'

'It wasn't haunted,' Meg pointed out.

'Might have been safer if it was,' Jonny said as he joined them.

'How much?' Art asked.

'A lot,' Jonny said. 'Much, much safer indeed.'

'He means how much money did we get,' Meg said.

A slight quiver of Jonny's mouth was the only sign that he had known this and was teasing them. 'Enough to make up the shortfall in last month's rent. And with what we have at the den, there's enough to pay the rent for this month,' he said with satisfaction.

'That will please Mr Jerrickson,' Art said. 'Flinch and I will take him this money now if he's in the shop. We can give him the rest later in the week. We'll meet you back at the den.'

Flinch grinned. She liked old Mr Jerrickson. Meg scowled, but that meant nothing. Her normal expression was more of a frown than a smile. Jonny nodded thoughtfully.

'Just be sure the spooks that haunt the old locksmith's shop don't get you,' he told Flinch, ruffling her hair and giving a ghostly laugh.

Flinch ducked out from under Jonny's arm and tried to grab him. But Jonny was already at the stairs. 'See you back at the den, Meg,' he shouted. 'Last one there's a rotten apple.'

'That's you, then, Meg,' Art said. 'You'll never catch Jonny.'

'No one ever catches Jonny,' Flinch agreed. 'He's the fastest.'

'Maybe,' Meg said, the ghost of a smile on her face. 'But I won't be the rotten apple.'

'Oh?'

'You two are off to see Mr Jerrickson. So I'll be at the den before either of you.'

The locksmith's shop was closed. But Flinch could see that there was a light on at the back and she guessed that Mr Jerrickson was still there. Art knocked on the door and, after a moment, the old man shuffled through from the back room.

The light from the nearest street lamp glinted on Mr Jerrickson's pebble-glasses as he opened the door and beckoned them in.

'I was just cutting a key for a customer,' he explained. 'He needs it first thing in the morning.'

They followed the little man through the shop and out to the back room. Art paused beside an old grandfather clock that stood against the wall and seemed to have stopped.

'Not brought Mr Lake with you, then?' Jerrickson asked them.

Like everyone else, he believed there really was a Brandon Lake, and that Art, Flinch, Jonny and Meg helped out and ran errands for him.

'He's busy this evening. Had to rush off,' Art explained.

Jerrickson nodded, not at all surprised. 'No doubt I'll meet the great man one day.'

'He's investigating a haunted theatre,' Flinch said. The thought of another mystery to solve excited her and she could not wait to get started.

'Is he now?'

'The Castle Theatre,' Flinch went on. 'There's spooky voices and strange sounds and everything.'

'Probably nothing to it,' Art said. But he smiled at Flinch, as if to add, 'But we'll have fun finding out.'

'The Castle Theatre,' Jerrickson said thoughtfully. He picked up the key he was working on and examined it. 'You know, I remember when Sir Carmichael built that place.' He rubbed carefully at the teeth of the key with a thin file. 'Just after the war, it was. He's supposed to have brought back the furnishings and most of the fixtures and fittings from some French château.'

'Hence the Castle Theatre,' Art said.

'That's right. Must have been 1919, I suppose. Of course, he was just plain Carmichael Rollason then. Didn't get his knighthood till much later.' He inspected the key again, comparing it with the original he was copying. 'Yes, that should do very nicely,' he decided. 'Now, you didn't come here to talk about theatres, haunted or otherwise, so how can I help you?'

'We brought the rent,' Flinch said. 'From Mr Lake.'

Art handed over the coins. 'That's what we

still owe for last month and something for this month too. We'll bring the rest later in the week, if that's all right.'

'That's fine, young man. Absolutely fine. Thank you. Trade picking up a bit, is it?' Jerrickson accepted the coins. He came round from behind his work table and went over to a small bureau in the corner of the room. 'I'll just put it in here for now. With the day's takings. For safekeeping.'

A small key from his pocket unlocked the bureau and Jerrickson folded down the front. Inside, Flinch could see several small drawers and pigeonholes. And something else. As Jerrickson moved, the light caught what looked like a pebble. It seemed almost to glow, colours swirling and changing on its surface.

'What's that?' Flinch asked in awe.

'This?' Jerrickson had put the money in one of the small drawers. He lifted the stone and held it out on the flat palm of his hand for Flinch to see. 'I really don't know. I found it months ago, on the floor in the room upstairs.' He was about to put it back again, but paused as a thought struck him. 'It isn't Mr Lake's, is it?'

'No.' Art's voice was firm. 'It used to be, but he doesn't want it any more,' he added as they turned to look at him. 'Really. You keep it, Mr Jerrickson. I'm sure he'd want you to have it.'

'Thank you.' Jerrickson looked again at the stone. 'Pretty thing. The way the colours catch the light . . .' Instead of putting it back in the bureau, he placed it on top, where it sparkled and shone. 'Seems a shame not to have it out where we can see it,' he said.

Art was unusually quiet on the way back to the den. Flinch talked about the haunted theatre and tried to get Art to tell her how they could find out if it really was haunted, but he seemed distracted and unwilling to talk.

'That stone Mr Jerrickson has,' Flinch said as they neared the warehouse, 'that's what's upset you, isn't it?'

'I'm not upset,' Art said sharply. Then he smiled and shook his head. 'Not really. I'm just . . .' He shrugged. 'I don't know. Seeing it again reminded me of Professor Bessemer and his paranormal puppets. That stone was what he used, somehow, to control them. It sort of focused his mind. Like using a magnifying glass to focus and increase the sun's rays so you can burn grass.'

Flinch frowned. 'Can you?'

'I'll show you some time. You remind me.'

'I will,' Flinch promised.

They were at the back of the warehouse now, within sight of the side door that they used to sneak inside. It was standing slightly open and Flinch thought she could see two eyes glinting in the darkness behind the door – watching them.

She was right. Almost at once, the door was pushed open and a figure charged out from the warehouse. She barely had time to realise it was Jonny before he was with them, walking back towards the door.

'What is it?' Art asked. 'What's the panic?'

'No panic,' Jonny said, 'but Charlie's here.'

Flinch almost bounced with joy at the news. She liked Charlie very much. He was, she thought, the oldest person she knew. But he was also one of the kindest. She loved his mass of white hair, the wrinkles round his eyes when he smiled and the way his eyes sparkled with interest at anything Flinch wanted to tell him. 'But it's not Tuesday,' she said.

Often on a Tuesday Charlie treated the children to tea at the Cannon Street station café. Occasionally they visited him in his huge house. His real name was Lord Fotherington, but to the children he had always been Charlie, and although he did not know the truth about the Invisible Detective, he had been involved in several mysteries.

Jonny held the door open for Flinch to go into the warehouse. He followed behind, letting Art bring up the rear and close the door behind them.

'So what does Charlie want?' Art asked. 'Or is it just a social call?'

'No,' Jonny said excitedly. 'He says he wants our help. Or rather the Invisible Detective's help. But he wouldn't say what it's about until you two were here as well.'

'I wonder what it can be,' Art said.

Flinch was impatient. She tugged at Art's sleeve to hurry him up. 'Let's go and ask him.'

'There is one other thing,' Jonny said. His expression was serious and his face was grave.

'What?' Flinch asked, suddenly worried by Jonny's abrupt change of manner.

'Yes, come on, Jonny,' Art said. 'What is it?'

'It's just that, well, Art . . .' Jonny's face cracked into a broad grin and he clapped Art on the shoulder. 'You're a rotten apple.'

There was a rip running diagonally down the middle of the page. Arthur Drake was sure he must have noticed it before. But that was the odd thing about reading the casebook of the Invisible Detective — it seemed as though he could only remember what he was supposed to. The rest simply slipped away, like a dream.

He dreamed about the Invisible Detective as well. Or rather about Meg and Jonny and Flinch. And about Art — who he now knew was his own grandfather. He found it strange that the boy of his own age who had written the casebook all those years ago in the 1930s was now in an old people's home. Grandad was fit and healthy enough, Arthur knew. His mind was still sharp. But he was old, and that brought frailty.

He did not seem to resent the fact that he

now needed help, that he was nowhere near as active as he had been. 'Happens to us all,' he had once remarked to his grandson, and with a sudden insight Arthur had realised he was right. They were so similar – they both had the same name and both their fathers were policemen (though Grandad's father was long since dead). Even their handwriting was identical, as the casebook bore witness. It had not struck Arthur before, but when he looked at Grandad he was seeing his own future. It seemed so very far off, old age. But it must have seemed the same to Grandad when, for example, he went to the Castle Theatre with his friends.

Arthur wondered, not for the first time, what had happened to Meg and Jonny, and to Flinch. Grandad was strangely reticent on the subject, but perhaps he simply did not know. Arthur and his school friend Sarah Bustle had tried to find some record of them on the Internet, but without success. Sarah knew about the Invisible Detective too, from her father. Though she had never really explained how her father knew, just shrugged off Arthur's questions and told him that her dad had never said. She lived with her mum and her young brother, Paul, now. Arthur could not recall ever meeting Sarah's dad — although his own father had known him well. Perhaps there was a connection there?

It was sad, he thought, as he pulled himself more upright in bed and ran his finger along the tear in the page of the casebook, but he was getting to the end of the book. He had read it all, he was sure. But he remembered only up to the adventure with the ancient Egyptian artefacts. An adventure that he and Sarah had been caught up in . . . At the moment he was reading about the business at the haunted Castle Theatre. It seemed vaguely familiar, but he was sure he should remember the section he had got to now.

The rip ran down the middle of the page for several inches, diagonally from left to right. It was a ragged line, the edges stained with ink. As if Art had purposefully dragged the pen down the page, pressing so hard it tore through the paper. But why?

The entry above was weird too. It started just like all the others — the date underlined: Saturday 24 April 1937. But under that, in the same handwriting which Arthur recognised as identical to his own, was written:

It's me, Arthur. I don't know how, but here I am. The performance is tomorrow and we have to stop it somehow.

I have a plan.

CHAPTER TWO

Dust hung in the air like mist. Art and the others were sitting on faded, decaying rolls of carpet, waiting for Charlie to explain.

'I'm not sure really what I am asking,' Charlie admitted. 'But it's a rum business and the War Office wants me to sort it out.'

Art leaned forward. 'Sort what out?'

'Well, that's just it. I'm not certain. But whatever is going on seems to me to be very much in Mr Lake's area of expertise rather than my own.'

This surprised Art. Charlie was not only a highly regarded adviser to the government, but one of the cleverest and most knowledgeable people he knew.

'Go on,' he said. 'I'm sure Mr Lake will be fascinated, as well as flattered.'

'I suppose,' Charlie said, 'there is no chance of communicating directly with the elusive Mr Lake?'

'None,' Meg told him.

'But we'll pass on the message,' Jonny said.

'It's like,' Flinch said slowly, 'if you tell us, you're telling him.'

'I assure you, every word will be relayed to Brandon Lake,' Art said.

Charlie nodded, thoughtful for a moment. He steepled his hands together as he considered what they had said. 'It is a very delicate matter. One that I have had to get the Prime Minister's approval to broach with Mr Lake.'

'You can trust us,' Flinch said at once, her eyes wide.

'I know,' Charlie told her. He looked round at the children, fixing each in turn with a solemn stare. 'But what I have to say is of the utmost secrecy. It must go no further than this room. It is for your ears only, and no one else's save Mr Lake himself.'

'We understand,' Art said.

'Good.' Charlie nodded with satisfaction. 'Then let me tell you that it seems more likely now than ever that within a very few years, possibly months, we may have to go to war.'

Flinch gasped. Meg looked shocked. But Jonny nodded as if he already knew that. Art felt his insides go cold. Of course, there had been talk of war, but talk was one thing.

'Obviously we all hope that such things can

be avoided,' Charlie was saying. 'But nevertheless there are certain preparations and precautions that must be made and taken. One of these is to make an accurate assessment of the efficiency and readiness of our military forces. A prudent measure, but one which must, of course, be kept absolutely secret.'

'You mean the results of the assessment or the fact it's being done?' Art wondered.

'I mean both. We cannot risk a potential enemy knowing our true strengths and weaknesses. But equally, we do not wish to be seen to be preparing for a war that we all of us hope to avoid. That very fact might indeed trigger the conflict if another country were to misinterpret our intentions. That is, after all, a large measure of what started the last war. The war to end all wars, or so we hoped.'

'So what's the problem?' Meg asked.

'Spies!' Flinch hissed.

'In a sense,' Charlie agreed. 'The assessment is being done secretly by a small group of officials under the chairmanship of Edward Watling. He is a senior civil servant at the War Office and the ideal man for the job. Until last week I would have said that he was ideally placed to make such an assessment and absolutely loyal and trustworthy.'

'So what happened last week?' Art asked.

The warehouse was silent as they waited for Charlie's reply. 'Watling attended a dinner,' he said. 'Luckily it was hosted by a colleague and friend of mine. Indeed, Watling is himself a friend of mine, which makes things slightly awkward and very bizarre. You see, I know him. So I know that what he did that evening was totally out of character.'

'And what did he do?' Meg asked impatiently.

'Towards the end of the dinner, he started reciting the preliminary findings of the assessment,' Charlie said. 'Out loud, at the dinner table, if you please. Didn't seem to care who heard him and wouldn't shut up.'

'What happened then?' Flinch asked in a loud whisper.

'My friend who was hosting the dinner led him out – still babbling secret information. He made light of it, said that Watling was unwell. It seems that most people there either took that at face value or realised the importance of not mentioning the event. We have contained things. For now at any rate.'

'And what does Watling say?' Art asked. 'What's his excuse?'

'Overwork?' Jonny suggested.

'Perhaps,' Charlie said. 'We have no way of knowing. The doctors say there is nothing wrong with him. And Watling himself refuses to believe that it ever happened. He maintains that there is no way he could have let slip even the slightest bit of information and can't understand what all the fuss is about. So far as he's concerned, the event never happened.'

'Except that it did,' Art said.

'No doubt of that,' Charlie told them. 'And the real dilemma is this: do we allow Watling to complete his assessment or not? He's the best man for the job, but what's to say he won't suddenly start spouting secret information again? Who knows what he might say, or who he might say it to?'

'So what have you done?' Art asked.

'Given him two weeks off, which I might say he's not terribly happy about. During that time, he's staying at my house, where at least I can keep an eye on him.' Charlie sighed. 'If the two weeks pass uneventfully, then I'd be inclined to drop the whole thing and pretend it never happened. But the matter is so sensitive, I must confess I am at a loss.'

'Can't you just get someone else to complete this report?' Jonny wanted to know.

'Indeed we could. But Watling has already done so much work. He already knows pretty much all there is to know. The damage, if indeed there is damage, has already been done, you see.'

'And he doesn't even know he's caused a problem?' Meg asked.

'Swears blind he never said a word. And I'm inclined to believe him.'

'What are you thinking, Meg?' Art asked, though he had a shrewd idea already.

'If he repeated that to me,' Meg said, 'I could tell if he's lying or if he really believes nothing happened. If that would help?' she added.

'It would set my mind at rest about poor Edward's trustworthiness at least,' Charlie said. 'Though it still leaves the question of what to do with him even if he is innocent but suffering some sort of illness.' Charlie stood up, looking round at them all. 'I'll tell you what, you inform Mr Lake of our discussions and get his opinion and suggestions. And then tomorrow, instead of tea at the café as usual, why don't you all come to my house?'

'Can we have cake?' Flinch asked at once, clapping her hands together in delight.

'Of course,' Charlie said with a smile. But it was a smile that did not quite reach his worried eyes. 'And I shall introduce you to my house guest, Mr Edward Watling.'

There was enough cake even for Flinch. Tea was served as always by Charlie's butler, Weathers. He knew the children well enough and made sure that everyone's cups and plates were never empty.

Edward Watling turned out to be a small, slightly rotund, middle-aged man. He was punctilious and polite and watched Flinch eat her cake with bemusement. But he never asked why she was so hungry or commented on her dishevelled appearance. He answered questions politely, but brushed off Art's enquiries about what he did for a living.

'Oh, I'm just a boring civil servant,' he told them. 'Not very exciting, I'm afraid. I always wanted to be a train driver when I was your age, but sadly that remains an unfulfilled ambition.'

'Are you staying with Charlie for long?' Jonny asked.

'That depends,' Watling confessed, 'on Charlie. He's looking after me, or so he says.'

'Are you ill?' Meg asked, setting down her teacup and watching the man closely.

'I don't think so. Just some nonsense idea of Charlie's.'

Charlie glanced at Meg, then said, 'Oh, come on, Edward. You did have a rather nasty turn at old Peter Simpson's the other night, didn't you?'

'Did I?' Watling shook his head. 'So you tell me. And Simpson too. But I don't remember a thing about it. I'm quite sure that Simpson made the whole thing up to embarrass me – you know what he's like. I probably upset him by not being enthusiastic enough about his wife's new dress or something. It's all quite, quite ridiculous. There's nothing wrong with me at all.' He smiled as if to prove how silly it all was, and held his cup out for Weathers to refill with tea.

'So you weren't taken ill or anything?' Meg asked carefully.

'Of course not. And I think I'm quite capable of looking after myself. But I must admit I'm grateful for the company. Normally, you see, I live on my own.'

Meg looked at Charlie and shook her head slightly. Art caught the gesture, and knew she meant that Watling was not lying. At least, he honestly believed himself to be telling the truth when he said there had not been a problem.

'Do you get lonely?' Flinch was asking. 'I live on my own, but I've got my friends.' She grinned at the others.

'Indeed, so have I,' Watling agreed. 'And with no one else relying on me I am free to work late if I need, or treat myself to the occasional trip to the theatre.'

'Ah, the theatre,' Charlie declared, as if glad to have a new subject to discuss. 'Now, you recall I was telling you about the elusive Brandon Lake, the associate of my friends here?'

Watling nodded his head enthusiastically. 'Indeed I do. It all sounds most intriguing.'

'Well, his latest mysterious case involves a theatre,' Charlie said. 'Or so Art tells me.'

'Indeed?'

'It's a haunted theatre,' Flinch said proudly, as if she owned it herself. 'There are spooky voices and witches and everything.'

'That sounds very different from the sorts of places I frequent,' Watling said. 'Unless you mean that these things happen on the stage?'

'No,' Jonny told him. 'Ghostly voices after it's all closed up. The cleaning ladies hear this voice whispering spells or something.'

'It's probably nothing,' Meg said. 'Just their imagination.'

'It's a witch,' Flinch declared, 'the ghost of a witch, and we're going to prove it, aren't we, Art?'

Art smiled, amused and pleased as always by Flinch's faith in him. '*By the pricking of my thumbs,*' he quoted from Shakespeare, '*something wicked this way comes.*' He turned to tell Watling that the Invisible Detective was on the case and that they would let him and Charlie know the outcome.

But Watling was sitting still as a statue, staring past Art's shoulder as if he could not see him. He blinked and his shoulders seem to jerk involuntarily. His teacup slipped from his fingers, crashing into the saucer on his lap. Both cup and saucer fell to the floor, spilling tea over the carpet. The saucer bounced once, then spun to a halt beside the cup. But Watling seemed not to notice at all.

When he spoke, Watling's voice was loud and clear but without expression – flat and unemotional. His eyes were still unfocused. 'At present we must conclude that British military forces are insufficient to mount a staunch mainland defence against attack by a hostile power,' Watling said in a monotone. 'We must assume a capability of fewer than twenty functioning infantry divisions, while armoured units are severely ill-equipped and likely to be overrun.'

Charlie got slowly to his feet, his face pale. 'Edward,' he said quietly, shaking Watling by the shoulder. 'Stop that at once, Edward.'

But Watling ignored him. 'Field and anti-tank artillery pieces are in short supply and all units are under-equipped. While the number of available tanks seems sufficient on paper, most are obsolete and only a fraction are actually of real combat value.'

Charlie nodded to Weathers and together they helped Watling to his feet. He seemed not to notice, but allowed himself to be led from the room, still reciting in a dull but precise manner the state of Britain's armed forces.

'He doesn't know he's doing it,' Meg said as soon as the door closed behind Charlie and the others. 'He really doesn't believe anything strange happened at that dinner party.'

'Well, if Charlie wanted proof that it did,' Art said, 'he's got it now.'

'But why is Watling doing it?' Jonny asked.

'Poor man,' Flinch said quietly. She picked up the discarded cup and saucer and put them on the low table beside her own.

Before long, Charlie was back. 'Weathers is with him,' he explained. 'From what Peter Simpson told me, there's no stopping him until he's been through the relative strengths – and weaknesses – of the army, the navy and the Royal Air Force. Well . . .' He sat down and reached for his tea, but put the cup down again without drinking any. 'I don't think there's much doubt that we have a problem.'

'We will tell Mr Lake what has happened,' Art said. 'Though, to be honest, I'm not sure what he'll be able to suggest.'

'Nor me,' Charlie confessed. 'But any ideas would be useful at this stage. I have to admit that I'm at a bit of a loss.' He shook his head. 'We can't just keep poor Watling incarcerated until his information is out of date. Could be years.' He sighed and stared off into the distance for several seconds. Then, with an obvious effort, he smiled. 'But I'm forgetting my manners. Is anyone else ready for another cup of tea?'

They talked for a few more minutes, but the conversation was overshadowed by the memory of Watling's strange behaviour, and Charlie was noticeably distracted. When the telephone began to ring, he was visibly startled from his reverie.

'Who can that be?' he wondered out loud, setting down his tea.

But before Charlie could get up, the ringing stopped. Weathers's measured voice was just audible from the hall outside, where there was another telephone. Art waited for Weathers to come into the drawing room to deliver a message. But instead they heard his footsteps moving away.

'Obviously not important,' Charlie decided, and returned to his tea.

Weathers appeared a short while later and

began to tidy away the tea things. Even Flinch had given up on the cake.

'Anything urgent?' Charlie asked Weathers as the butler took his plate and cup.

'I'm sorry, sir?'

'The telephone.'

'No, sir. That is, it was a call for Mr Watling.'

Charlie nodded. 'We had to leave a contact number for him at the office, of course,' he explained to Art and the others. 'Did you say that Mr Watling was indisposed?'

'He seemed to have recovered, sir,' Weathers told them. 'Doesn't seem aware that there was a problem even. He was quite surprised to find himself in his room, in fact.'

'That fits with what Simpson told me,' Charlie said. 'Thank you, Weathers.'

'Sir.' Weathers paused, then added, 'It wasn't his office, though, sir. Apparently it was a message from his sister.'

Charlie frowned. 'His sister?' he echoed, clearly puzzled.

'What is it?' Meg asked.

In the brief silence, the sound seemed even louder. Like a gunshot. Flinch gave a gasp of surprise, Meg and Jonny both turned. It took Art a moment to realise what he had heard – the slam of the front door closing. Weathers was already hurrying out of the room, into the hallway.

Art looked back at Charlie, who was still sitting white-faced in front of them.

'Watling doesn't have a sister,' Charlie said quietly.

Weathers was back in moments, breathless from running upstairs and checking out in the driveway. 'I'm sorry, sir,' he said to Charlie. 'But Mr Watling's gone.'

Charlie bade them goodbye, apologising for the fact that he had some telephoning of his own to do. Meg was keen to get home and, since the den was on her way, Flinch went with her. Jonny and Art could take a short cut back from Charlie's and said goodbye to the girls at the corner of the street.

'I suppose he must be a spy after all,' Jonny said as they walked.

'And that telephone call was a message to say that his accomplices had arranged for his escape,' Art agreed. 'All a bit odd, though.'

'He was well placed to get information. Perhaps they offered him a lot of money.'

'No, I mean the way he just recited that report,' Art said. 'I mean, if you were a spy, you wouldn't want everyone knowing you were a spy, would you? And Meg said he didn't know he'd done it.'

Jonny shrugged. 'That's it, then.'

'What?'

'It's like a guilty conscience. He can't control it, but he keeps giving himself away.'

'I suppose it's possible,' Art said. But he didn't sound convinced.

When they reached the point where Art and Jonny needed to head in different directions, Jonny turned to say goodbye. Art was standing thoughtfully.

'The police will soon find Watling,' Jonny said. 'They'll have the ports covered and everything.'

In the distance a clock was chiming.

'Dad's working tonight,' Art said. 'You don't need to be home yet, do you?'

'I suppose not.' Jonny gave a short laugh. 'You don't think we'll find him before the police do?'

'Of course not.' Art laughed too. 'I just

wondered if you fancied making a bit of a detour. To Carshalton Street.'

'Why?'

Art's eyes widened, and when he spoke his voice was deep, booming and almost ghostly. 'To take a look at a haunted theatre,' he said.

The Castle Theatre dominated the end of Carshalton Street. It did indeed look like a small castle. The top of the building was adorned with mock battlements and the whole of the frontage was faced with rough stone. A short flight of steps led up to an imposing arched doorway. There were two large barred windows on the ground floor, but none at all in the upper part of the building. Instead there were gaps in the stonework, intended to look like arrow slits.

'You don't want to go inside, do you?' Jonny asked nervously. 'There's probably a performance still on.'

'That's all right,' Art assured him. 'I just wanted to take a look at the place. Anyway,' he added with a grin, 'they'd probably drop boiling oil down on us from the battlements as soon as we got too close.'

They both laughed at this. But their laughter changed to a moment's anxiety as the heavy wooden doors suddenly swung open. Jonny stepped back into the shadow of a doorway, pulling Art with him.

'It's just the end of the show,' Art said.

The first people from the audience were coming out of the theatre now, laughing and discussing the show in loud voices.

'I bet everyone who lives here loves it,' Jonny commented.

There was a steady stream of people down the street, past the doorway where Art and Jonny stood and watched. The boys caught odd snatches of conversation, brief comments as people passed:

'That conjuror . . .'

'. . . the thing with the onion . . .'

'. . . must taste horrible . . .'

'. . . haven't laughed so much in years . . .'

'Look!' This last was a sudden shout in Jonny's ear. Art had grabbed his shoulder and was pointing across the road.

'What is it?'

Jonny followed the line of Art's finger. But all he could see was the mass of people sweeping past.

'There, on the other side of the road. Just standing there.'

Jonny looked again, standing on tiptoes and struggling to see over the heads of the people. He was on a step slightly raised from the pavement and could just make out a figure standing motionless on the other side of the street. For a split second there was a gap in the rush of people from the theatre and he saw clearly who it was. He gave a gasp of surprise.

'Come on,' Art shouted, pulling Jonny after him and plunging into the crowd.

It was like swimming against a strong current. They pushed and shoved, shouted and barged, forcing their way across the road. It seemed to take for ever, and more than once Jonny felt himself stumble and was afraid he would fall and be trampled to death. But the crush of the people kept him upright.

At last Jonny emerged from the crowd. He looked round for Art and saw that he was standing where they had seen the figure. The figure who was now gone.

'It was him,' Art insisted. 'I know it was. Did you see him?'

Jonny nodded. 'Edward Watling. Just for a second. But it was him all right.'

'What was he doing here?'

'I guess he'd just come out of the theatre with everyone else.'

'But it doesn't make sense,' Art said. 'Why would a man wanted for spying and on the run from the police go to a show at the Castle Theatre?'

Arthur called in on his grandad after school the next day. He had the casebook in his bag and took it out to show Grandad the ripped page.

Grandad ran his finger down the tear, just as Arthur had done the previous night. Unlike Arthur's, Grandad's finger was crooked and wrinkled. The skin looked incredibly dry and the finger seemed to be all bone. It trembled as it moved.

'Yes,' Grandad said at last. 'Yes, I remember that I wondered about that too.' But he would not be drawn further. He closed the book and patted the cover affectionately. 'Some time I must borrow this and read it,' he said. 'Though it doesn't do to dwell on the past, it's nice to visit it now and again. I keep some photographs, a few odds and ends. Not much. To remind me.'

Arthur nodded. 'There are things in the book too,' he said. He opened it again to the ripped page and turned forward. 'Like this.'

There was a card glued into the book. It was faded and mottled with age, but the printing on it was clear enough:

A Special Performance of
William Shakespeare's acclaimed play

Macbeth

At the Castle Theatre, Carshalton Street
On Sunday 25 April
At 7.30 p.m.
By Invitation Only
Admit One

Grandad peered at the lettering and nodded. 'A performance to remember,' he said. 'By all accounts.'

'Didn't you go?'

Grandad smiled at him. 'Yes and no. In a manner of speaking.'

'What do you mean?'

'You'll find out.' As if to make the point that the matter was closed, Grandad handed Arthur back the book. 'The Castle Theatre,' he said quietly. 'Now, what did I see about that recently?' He tapped his fingers on the arm of his chair. 'Yes, local paper,' he decided. 'It must be around here somewhere.'

Arthur retrieved it from beside the bed. Nowhere much to lose anything in Grandad's small room, he reflected. There was a bed on which he was perched, a small armchair where Grandad was sitting, a table supported by a metal stand on one side so it could be moved over the bed, and a small display cabinet with drawers beneath. The wardrobes were built in round the bed, making the room seem even smaller.

The paper, Arthur saw without surprise, was folded to the crossword. Grandad took the paper from him and opened it out. He scanned the front page, then turned to the inside. After a minute he found what he was looking for.

'Here it is,' he said, refolding the paper and

looking at the article he had discovered. 'They've been renovating some of the buildings on Carshalton Street.'

'Carshalton Street? That's where the theatre was.'

'And still is, seemingly. Derelict, hidden away behind some new frontage or other, converted to offices during the war, then abandoned and forgotten.' He handed the paper to Arthur, jabbing at the article with his finger.

'And they're going to restore it,' Arthur saw as he skimmed through the piece. 'Restore the Castle Theatre and perform plays there again.'

'You'll see,' Grandad said, 'after that blather about it being architecturally important and of great interest that they've almost finished the restoration work. Apparently it was on the telly a few years back, though I can't say I noticed.'

There was mention, Arthur saw, of a series about saving old buildings. People phoned in and voted for the building they thought should get funding to restore it to its former glory. The Castle Theatre had not won, but it had generated sufficient interest and donations since for it to be renovated.

'It opens next week,' he said as he reached the end of the article.

Grandad was nodding. 'With a performance of *Macbeth*.'

'Coincidence?' Arthur wondered.

Grandad took back the paper. 'I doubt it. They mention the original performance as a high point in the theatre's life. There's irony for you,' he added with a wry smile. 'I suppose the point is that this is a return to the theatre's glory days. But I doubt if any two reviewers could agree on the merits of the original performance.'

CHAPTER THREE

Flinch didn't care that it wasn't proper theatre. She enjoyed every moment of the show. She couldn't understand why Meg was so rude about it. Back at the den that morning, Meg had made it very clear that she did not believe 'a variety show', as she called it, counted as a trip to the theatre. But as far as Flinch was concerned, a show was far more entertaining than some stuffy play. It was her first trip to the theatre and she was determined to make the most of it.

There was a more practical reason why Art was happy for Meg not to join them. There was only enough money saved for three tickets. Jonny had offered to miss the show, but it was obvious he wanted to go really. So Meg's decision was not one that Art or the others argued with.

Meg's only moment of slight regret had seemed to be when Art suggested that, as she had the afternoon free, she might like to go to the locksmith's and apologise to Mr Jerrickson for the fact that the Invisible Detective was spending the rest of the rent he had promised on Monday night on a theatre trip for Art, Jonny and Flinch.

That did not worry Flinch. They would soon get more money from the consulting sessions, and she was sure that Mr Jerrickson would not mind at all. She could imagine his spectacles sparkling almost as much as his eyes as he told Meg not to worry and that if his money was going towards helping with another important investigation then that was fine by him.

Not that it seemed much like an investigation, Flinch thought. The Castle Theatre ran four shows a day, starting in the early afternoon and finally closing at half-past ten at night. Each of the shows lasted about an hour and a half, including a short interval, and there was a half-hour break between them to allow the existing audience out and the next one in. Flinch imagined that it also gave the performers a chance for a break. There were so many acts, she lost count. There were several singers, a brass band, dancers, jugglers and a group of acrobats. There was a man who played tunes by blowing into a copper kettle. But the two acts that caught Flinch's imagination the most were the magician and the hypnotist.

The magician was called Prester Digitation, which Art for some reason found funny. He could make boiled eggs appear from his mouth and coins disappear into thin air. He could produce streams of silk handkerchiefs from the top pocket of his jacket, and he could tell people in the audience what cards they had chosen when he wasn't looking. He made things vanish from a table on the other side of the stage – his assistant covering it with a cloth and then whipping it off to reveal the trick while the magician stayed well away, pulling thoughtfully at the ends of his impressive moustache. He produced a fluffy white rabbit from inside his hat. There was applause at this, followed by a loud shout from somewhere behind Flinch.

'Now eat the rabbit!'

Flinch swung round in her seat and glared, though she could not tell who had called out. Lots of people were laughing, which seemed unfair, but the magician had already made the rabbit disappear again.

To finish with, Prester Digitation first sawed his assistant in half – getting her to lie inside a coffin-like box while he cut through it. Then, when he had pushed the two halves of the box back together and helped the young woman out again, apparently none the worse for the experience, he announced his final trick.

It was a display of mind-reading and would lead, the magician said, into the next act – the last and, Flinch expected, the most impressive in the show: the hypnotist.

It was a good trick. The magician's assistant came down into the audience. People whispered to her the names of cards and on the stage Mr Digitation concentrated on their minds until he knew what card they had chosen. Then he produced it with a flourish from the pack and held it up for everyone to see. The people who had chosen the cards laughed and nodded and clapped and gasped along with the rest of the audience.

Then finally, the magician asked for a number. A number between one and a hundred – no, he decided, between one and a thousand. His assistant, who was called Eve, walked along the aisle looking for someone to ask for the number. Flinch stuck her hand in the air and bounced on her seat, ignoring Art and Jonny's amusement. Eve walked close by them, past the end of their row of seats, but she didn't ask Flinch.

Flinch was disappointed. She was disappointed

not to be asked, and also because she could see as Eve passed close by that the assistant was not as young as she seemed. She might be wearing a short, sequinned skirt and smiling through young make-up, but the powder on her face was thinning now and there were wrinkles round her eyes. Another illusion, Flinch thought. The woman looked as old as Meg's mother.

But then Eve made the man she had chosen write his number down on a card, and the magician concentrated, and the theatre fell silent.

'One hundred and ninety-nine,' Prester Digitation announced in a loud clear voice.

In the expectant hush, Eve held up the card. And there, written large and bold, was '199'. There was a roar of applause. Eve ran back to the stage. And as she reached it, the magician took a bow, twirled his moustache and disappeared in a sudden explosion of smoke and noise. When the smoke thinned, Flinch could see that only the magician's top hat remained on the stage. She laughed and clapped and shouted with Art and Jonny.

The hypnotist was much quieter than the magician and he had no assistant. He was, according to the board at the side of the stage that announced the acts, 'The Great Giuseppe of Naples, Italian Master of Hypnosis and Mesmerism'. Flinch found his act fascinating, but a little creepy.

Giuseppe was a short man with oiled black hair and a small moustache that was far less impressive than the magician's. He spoke with a strange accent which Jonny whispered to Flinch was Italian. He selected people from the ends of rows in the audience to come up on stage and be hypnotised. They all seemed to agree to this more easily than Flinch would have done.

Especially once she saw what happened to the people. The hypnotist looked into their eyes and spoke with a quiet, calm voice laced richly with his Italian accent. He told them things that were obviously not true and yet the people believed him. Giuseppe told the first man that he was a chicken. Within moments the man was parading up and down the stage with his chin thrust forward and his arms working like wings at his sides. He clucked and strutted and at one point actually seemed to think he had laid an egg. Even after he was turned back into himself and sent to his seat, he emitted the occasional involuntary cluck during moments of silence.

Several people became a train which processed around the theatre, making chuff-chuff sounds and whistling. Flinch thought that was funny, but she still felt uneasy at the way people could be made to do such things.

The last person the hypnotist called up was a large, red-haired man with broad shoulders and an enormous stomach. The hypnotist looked at him, and seemed to decide that he did not want to make a fool of someone so big. It might not turn out too well for him, he admitted, and he sent the man back to his seat. 'Oh, and here's a nice, red, juicy apple for your trouble,' he said.

The large man seemed happy with this, and celebrated his victory by taking a huge bite from the apple even before he was off the stage. Then he congratulated Giuseppe on what a tasty apple it was.

Except that Flinch and everyone else could see that it wasn't an apple at all. It was an onion. Yet the man bit chunks out of it and munched away happily as the audience applauded and the curtain came down.

People round Art, Jonny and Flinch were getting up, pulling on their coats, pushing their way along the row of seats and making for the doors. But Art gestured for Jonny and Flinch to stay seated.

'We'll wait for it to clear out a bit,' he said. 'Then let's see if we can get backstage and have a look round.'

'You think Edward Watling might still be here, hiding?' Jonny asked.

'We could search,' Flinch suggested.

Art shook his head. 'It will be too busy. There's another performance in half an hour or so, remember. But I'd like to see the corridor where Mary Foster heard the ghostly voice.'

'Do you think we'll hear the ghost?' Flinch wondered.

'I doubt we'll hear anything apart from people getting ready for the next show,' Jonny said. 'But you never know.'

'That hypnotist is spooky,' Flinch said.

'Yes,' Art agreed. 'Yes, he is.'

Meg helped her mother with the washing before she went to the locksmith's. Like Flinch, she was sure that Mr Jerrickson would not mind that they were late again with the rent money, but she still felt embarrassed and put off the meeting until she really had nothing else to do.

She had waited so long that the show must be almost over by now, Meg thought. The others had said they would meet her back at the den after the performance. Probably she would have enjoyed seeing the various acts, but Meg just wasn't in the mood. She had enjoyed the time spent with her mother, and Flinch would tell her all about the theatre trip, she was sure.

There was a bell fixed inside the door, positioned so that the door just nudged it as it opened. The bell rang when Meg came into the shop and Mr Jerrickson's cracked voice called out from the back room, 'Be with you in a moment.'

'It's only me – Meg.' But as soon as she said it, the door opened again, catching Meg in the back and forcing her to take a quick step forwards.

'Then come on through,' Mr Jerrickson called.

Rather than shout out again, Meg went through, conscious of the other customer following close behind her. She glanced back and saw that it was a figure wrapped in a large, heavy coat and with a trilby hat pulled down low. The face was all but covered with a muffler and in a gloved hand the figure was holding a large, old-fashioned-looking key.

'You have a customer,' Meg said as soon as she stepped into the back room.

Jerrickson looked up from his work and nodded politely. 'Key is it?' He held out his hand and took the key. He smiled at Meg to assure her that he would not be long. 'Problem?' he enquired, examining the key. 'Or do you need a duplicate?'

The customer had turned away and seemed to be inspecting the cluttered room with interest. 'Two duplicates,' came the reply – a low, dry, rasping voice. 'It's urgent.'

'You can wait if you like. But it will be a couple of hours before I can get them finished. Some other jobs to complete for this evening,' Jerrickson explained apologetically. He was already hunting for a blank key of the same design. 'Looks simple enough, though. For a door, is it?'

The figure nodded curtly. It was standing beside the bureau at the side of the room. Meg could see the strange stone from the Invisible Detective's encounter with Professor Bessemer's Paranormal Puppet Show was resting on top of the bureau. It caught the light and glimmered in a myriad of colours. But the customer seemed to ignore it, turning back towards Jerrickson. And Meg was already thinking about something else.

'Yes, a door,' came the rasping reply.

It seemed to Meg that whoever it was had deliberately disguised their voice. What were they hoping to hide? She was sure it was no one she knew. The figure turned back towards the bureau. Meg was wondering why the customer had lied. It was indeed the key to a door – that had been true enough. But Meg knew from the way they had said it, knew for certain, that the job was not urgent at all.

So why say that it was?

She was still wondering when the customer agreed to return the next morning and went back to the main shop. The bell at the door rang again as they left, and Mr Jerrickson smiled at Meg.

'And what can I do for you, my dear?' he asked.

*

It was easy enough to find a door that led to the area behind the stage. Art thought it would be just as simple to have a look round without attracting attention. There would be many people backstage, getting ready for the next performance. They would assume that the three children were meant to be there – especially if Art and Jonny and Flinch looked confident and behaved as if they knew where they were going and what they were doing.

Certainly it was busy. Everyone seemed to know exactly what they were about, which had the opposite effect from what Art had hoped. Because they were so used to the routine of preparing for the next show, everyone immediately noticed the strangers.

'Who are you?' one of the band asked Art. 'What do you want?'

'Yes,' a juggler agreed, 'can we help? Looking for someone?'

'Er, I was looking for Giuseppe, the hypnotist,' Art said quickly.

The woman who had sung 'Daisy, Daisy' in such a raucous manner was pushing past them in the narrow corridor. She laughed like a seal being machine-gunned. 'You won't see him. He'll be closeted in his dressing room, preparing for the next show.'

Art could not imagine what preparation was needed – apart from finding another onion. Did he have to practise in front of the mirror perhaps – get his mind into a certain state?

'Or the magician,' Flinch said. 'I'd like to see Mr Digitation.'

'Eve's got her claws into him,' the singer laughed. 'I doubt you'll see him either.'

'You won't see no one if Gregson finds you first,' the juggler said. He was a tall, thin man of about twenty with a kindly face. 'If he catches you larking about back here . . .' He stopped mid-sentence, looking suddenly rather pale.

'Who's Gregson?' Jonny asked the juggler.

But the man did not reply. He seemed about to speak, then changed his mind, turned and walked quickly away.

'I'm Gregson.' The voice was harsh and angry and came from behind them. It belonged, Art saw when he turned, to a large man with thinning grey hair. He had a cigar clamped between his teeth and seemed to speak round it.

His face was bulbous, with saggy jowls, and his expression was one of thunderous anger. 'I'm Algernon Makepeace Gregson and I'm the manager of this theatre. So I hope you've got a damned good reason to be here, interrupting my routine and my performers.'

Art swallowed. He could see that Jonny was ready to run at the slightest sign from him. Only Flinch did not seem intimidated.

'I want to see the magician,' she announced.

Gregson's face seemed to ripen into a rich red colour. The cigar twitched angrily.

'And his rabbit,' Flinch added.

They did run after that. Gregson's threats about what he would do if he ever saw them hanging round his theatre again rang in their ears as they raced down Carshalton Street. Jonny was kind enough not to run too far ahead, and eventually let Flinch and Art catch up with him.

'There was no call for that sort of language,' he said.

Art was out of breath. 'That theatre is haunted, we know that,' he gasped. 'But not by a ghost. By Algernon Makepeace Gregson.'

'I didn't like that man,' Flinch said with her usual simplicity and directness.

'That's all right,' Jonny told her. 'Neither did we.'

'And I don't think he really cared for us,' Art agreed. 'Though maybe that's just my impression.'

Their nervousness had been replaced by amusement by the time they got back to the den. They were laughing as they made their way through to the main area and saw that Meg was there already.

She was not alone. Charlie was sitting on one of the rolls of carpet, examining his hat with a grave expression.

'I saw Mr Jerrickson,' Meg told Art. 'And then I got back here to find Charlie waiting for us. He's . . .' She paused and glanced at Charlie, who was getting to his feet. He looked tired and suddenly very old. 'He's got some news for us,' Meg finished.

'What is it?' Flinch asked quietly.

'About Edward Watling?' Jonny guessed.

He glanced at Art, obviously wondering if they should tell Charlie they had seen the man the previous evening.

Art shook his head. Not now. 'You've found him?' he asked.

'Yes,' Charlie said. 'We've found him. He turned up at his office for work this morning as if nothing untoward had taken place.'

They all sat round and listened to Charlie as he told them briefly what had happened.

'He went to his desk as usual and started on his paperwork. His secretary, who has some idea of what's going on, phoned me and I went round there at once.'

'And did you find him?' Art said.

Charlie shook his head. 'I got there about half-past ten. But I was too late. By then it was all over.'

'All over?' Jonny said. 'What happened?'

'It seems that Watling worked for about an hour, apparently perfectly normally. No sign of anything wrong. Then, at about ten o'clock, he took a telephone call. His secretary doesn't know who from. Watling said nothing. He just listened for a short time, then replaced the receiver . . .'

'What happened next?' Flinch wanted to know.

'Watling got up from his desk, smiled at his

secretary, opened the large window in his office
. . . and jumped out.'

There were gasps from them all at this.

'But why?' Jonny said.

'He wasn't making a run for it?' Art asked
quietly.

Charlie was shaking his head sadly. 'His
office,' he said, 'is on the thirteenth floor. He died
instantly.'

'Why don't we go and look?' Sarah suggested.

They were walking out of school together, as
they often did. Sarah was actually in the year above
Arthur, but they finished at the same time.

'At the Castle Theatre?'

She shrugged, her head to one side so that her
long black hair hung away from her oval face. 'Why
not?'

It won't be open,' Arthur pointed out.

'They'll be finishing the restoration work or
whatever, won't they? They're putting a play on in a
few days. There will be people there.'

Arthur wasn't sure, though he had to admit he would like to see the theatre. The casebook was strangely coy about the events that had taken place there in the 1930s. He had asked Grandad why he hadn't written them up in more detail, but the old man simply smiled and said, 'Perhaps I didn't feel qualified.'

'It can't do any harm,' Sarah continued. 'Or do you have to get home?'

'No, Dad's working. There's no rush.'

They were at the gates now.

'Well, then?'

It looked as if there was still a lot to do. There were several skips in the road outside the theatre. The houses that had once lined Carshalton Street were gone. On one side was a block of offices – steel and smoked glass. On the other there was a health club – a large, boring, red-brick building with a sign outside advertising the size of the swimming pool and offering a deal on annual membership.

A large grey van was parked outside the theatre, cables running from the back of it towards the building. As Arthur and Sarah approached, a television camera team backed out of the main entrance, one man holding the camera braced on his shoulder, another with a long furry microphone. A young woman with straggly hair and a clipboard walked beside them. They were all watching the man who followed them confidently out of the building. His teeth flashed in the sunlight as he smiled over-enthusiastically.

'It's that TV guy,' Sarah said.

'You don't say.'

'You know, Miles thingy.'

'Kershaw,' Arthur told her.

Miles Kershaw hosted all manner of TV programmes. He had done the National Lottery show for a while as well, Arthur remembered. He had a reputation for being matey and honest and one of 'the people'.

They watched as the television crew finished. Miles Kershaw flashed several more trademark smiles, raised his eyebrows as he ad-libbed some witty asides, and patted the woman with the clipboard on the shoulder when they were finished. She did not react.

Then Kershaw caught sight of Sarah and Arthur watching from beside the van. His smile faded and a scowl took over. He muttered something to the woman, who glanced over at Sarah and Arthur and shrugged. Clearly not satisfied with this, Kershaw wiped his unnaturally dark hair back into place with the flat of his hand and marched towards them.

'He's coming this way.' Sarah sounded impressed.

Arthur was less excited. 'Don't ask for his autograph, for goodness' sake.'

Kershaw's familiar voice reached them before he did. 'Are you kids meant to be here?' he demanded. 'You should be in school.'

'School's over,' Arthur told him. 'We were just watching.'

'We're interested in the Castle Theatre,' Sarah said. 'We'd love to see it.'

Kershaw seemed to soften at her words. 'Really? Interested, eh?' He raised an immaculate eyebrow. 'Like to see it, would you?'

'Please.'

'Then watch it on the telly,' Kershaw snapped. 'Next Monday, eight p.m. Now – scram.'

'We can watch if we want,' Arthur said. He didn't like Kershaw even when he was being his usual unctuous self. 'We've every right to be here. Keep your hair on.'

For a moment, Kershaw looked stunned. His hand flew to his head, and Arthur stifled a laugh as he realised why the man's hair always seemed so well groomed.

To his credit, Kershaw recovered almost at once. 'Listen, sonny,' he said with mock politeness, 'there are a lot of very busy people in there with a lot of work to do. I'm sure they would deem it a favour if you didn't interrupt them. So keep well out of the way. Unless you want me to make an official complaint.'

Arthur was half minded to ask who Kershaw was intending to complain to, officially. But the man had already stalked away, heading back towards the theatre.

'Come on,' Sarah said, turning to go.

'Not likely,' Arthur told her. He wasn't going to let some smarmy TV bloke tell him what to do. 'Let's take a look inside. The door's open.'

'But you heard what he said.'

'You want to see what it's like inside too, don't you?' He grinned at her. 'Or do you have to get home?'

Sarah did not smile back. 'Come on, then,' she said.

*

It was incredible how like an actual castle the building was. Arthur had read descriptions in the casebook, but even the exterior had not prepared him for the real thing.

Huge double doors opened into the foyer, which was full of people. The floor was covered with dustsheets to protect it while painters painted, polishers polished the woodwork, masons were attending to the stone walls, and other workmen came and went. Arthur could begin to appreciate Miles Kershaw's point. Even in among all the activity, he could see the castle theme continued through-out. Edges of huge flagstones poked out where the dustsheets left patches of floor uncovered; the walls were apparently built from large stone blocks; the woodwork was a careful blend of the ornate and the functional.

'There must be another way in,' Sarah said.

'Stage door,' Arthur suggested. 'Though it may be as busy back there.'

'I doubt it,' Sarah said as they made their way round to the side of the theatre. 'It opens next week, so they should be nearly finished. If I was planning it, I'd do the foyer last.'

'Why?'

'Because that's where everyone goes traipsing through, making a mess while they're restoring the rest of the place.'

The stage door was wedged open, perhaps to let air in and dust out. As soon as they stepped inside, Arthur could see that Sarah was right. The backstage area seemed pretty much finished. White plaster dust coated everything, though in places he could see where someone had tried to wipe it away. Some of the stonework looked slightly pale, and he guessed there were new parts replacing areas that had become damp or damaged.

The emptiness of the corridor that led down past the dressing rooms was a contrast to the crowded, noisy foyer. Sarah pushed open a door to reveal a bare room. There was a mirror fixed to the wall, and a narrow window at the end of the room afforded a view of the brick wall outside. There was no furniture, and the floor in here was bare, unpolished wooden boards.

'This is pretty boring,' Sarah decided.

'Let's see if we can get to the stage.'

They found their way with no problem. But a group of carpenters were using the stage as a workshop – cutting wood on trestles and staining finished carvings. At the end of the stage closest to Arthur and Sarah, a statue of a female figure stood. She was life-sized, and Arthur was amazed at the intricacy of the carving. She looked almost real, except for the fact that she was dark polished wood and you could see the grain in her features. There was a strange half-smile on her lips. She was dressed in a long flowing robe, every fold and crease carefully shaped. Her arms were bare, raised above her head as if she was carrying something, except there was nothing there.

'A caryatid,' Sarah said quietly.

'A what-id?'

'It's like a pillar. She holds up a roof or a lintel or something. There was a question from the Invisible Detective website about classical architecture the other week,' she added with a smile.

As she was speaking, two men came over and between them pushed the woman on to her side and lifted her up.

'Where's this one for?' one of the men asked. 'Auditorium?'

'No,' the other man said. 'Main bar. Upstairs.'

The first man grimaced as he hefted the heavy figure. 'Would be, wouldn't it?' he grumbled.

'Come on,' Sarah said to Arthur. 'I think we've seen enough.'

'I suppose so. Once they're finished, it'll probably be open to the public anyway.'

They had reached the dressing room corridor when they heard the clear and distinctive voice of Miles Kershaw: 'So let's see just how they're getting on in the main theatre, shall we?'

Arthur and Sarah stopped and looked at each other.

'And I think we'll be surprised at just how much progress has been made in so short a time,' Kershaw went on.

'He sounds like he's on the telly,' Sarah whispered.

'He is,' Arthur told her. 'And we'll be on the telly too if we don't move it!'

'They're coming this way,' Sarah realised.

Together they ran in the opposite direction – down the corridor and deeper into the building.

'Where are we going?' Sarah gasped.

The corridor turned a corner and they slowed to a quick walk.

'There must be another way out. Mustn't there?'

'I'm not so sure.'

They passed more doors – offices and store-rooms. Ahead of them, the corridor ended in a flight of stone steps leading down into darkness.

'We can't get out that way,' Sarah protested. 'It's just the cellar.'

'I don't think I want to try,' Arthur admitted. 'It's haunted.'

Sarah just stared at him. 'Yeah,' she said. 'Right.'

'So let's wait here a bit, then sneak back when Kershaw and the others have gone.'

Sarah nodded. But before she could reply, they both heard Kershaw's voice echoing along the corridor after them: 'But first we're going to take a look at what's been done to renovate even the simplest office or storeroom . . .'

'Haunted cellar it is,' Sarah said. 'Come on.'

CHAPTER FOUR

Art heard about the break-in from his father at breakfast the next morning. Dad had been working most of the night and had only just got in when Art was getting ready for school.

'I was round at your friend Mr Jerrickson's last night,' he told Art as he passed him a plate of bacon and eggs. 'Poor chap was a bit shaken up.'

'What happened?'

Art's dad sat opposite him at the table. He stretched and yawned. 'Nothing too serious luckily. His shop was broken into during the night.'

'Oh, no.' Suddenly Art did not feel hungry. He put down his fork. 'Was much taken?'

'Nothing at all, that's the strange thing.' Dad had not lost his appetite and was shovelling bacon into his mouth. He paused to slosh some tea in as well. 'We think maybe they were disturbed. A window was broken, so perhaps someone heard the noise. They got scared and ran off.'

'You think they'll come back?' Art wanted to know.

'Oh, I doubt it. Probably a spur of the moment thing. They'll try somewhere else next time.'

Art picked up his fork and had another go at the breakfast. 'That was lucky.'

Dad nodded. 'Mr Jerrickson's going to check and let me know for sure, but it seems there's nothing missing. Well,' he added through a mouthful of egg, 'nothing important.' Dad yawned again. 'I'm all done in. It's been a long night.' He smiled at Art. 'Guess I need some sleep. You mind washing up?'

'Of course not.'

'No,' Dad said as he stood up from the table. 'Nothing missing except some strange stone that Jerrickson was going on about. Can't see why he's so worried about it, though. Seems to me he had a lucky escape.'

By the time he had finished washing up, Art had to hurry to get to school. So he had to wait the whole day until he could get to the locksmith's shop to see Mr Jerrickson. All day he wondered about the stone – it had to be the one he and Flinch had seen Mr Jerrickson put out on top of the bureau. The one that had controlled Professor Bessemer's strange puppets. His mind was racing, making all sorts of connections – Edward

Watling, the Castle Theatre, ghostly voices, a stage hypnotist, the break-in . . .

At the end of school he ran to the den. It was on the way to Jerrickson's and he hoped the others would be there already, but in fact there was only Meg. She was sitting on one of the dusty rolls of carpet, reading a book.

'Jonny and Flinch went to watch the ships on the river,' she said. 'I wanted to finish this.'

She returned her attention to the book. Art could see that she only had a few pages left, but he couldn't bear to wait.

'Can you leave it for a minute?' he asked.

Meg glanced up at him, her lips tight and her head tilted to one side. Art expected her to tell him in no uncertain terms that, no, she couldn't leave it. But she must have seen something in his own expression, or caught a hint of the anxiety in his voice. She pushed a postcard she was using as a bookmark in between the pages and closed the book.

'What is it?'

Art sat down beside her. 'Mr Jerrickson's shop was broken into last night.' He held up his hands to stem her worried questions. 'Nothing was taken, according to Dad. Nothing, that is, except a strange stone that Mr Jerrickson had.'

Meg just stared at him. 'It was on top of that little desk that closes up, in the back room,' she said. 'I saw it yesterday. Are you sure that's what was taken?'

'Seems most likely,' Art said with a shrug. 'I was just on my way to ask him.'

Meg was on her feet. 'Come on, then,' she said.

Leaving her book on the roll of carpet, she ran with Art to the back door of the old warehouse.

There was a sheet of plywood over one of the glass panels in the door of the locksmith's. Mr Jerrickson was in the main part of the shop and he looked up warily as they entered. But he smiled when he saw who it was. He appeared tired and worn.

'Dad told me what happened,' Art said. 'We just wanted to check you were all right.'

'It's awful,' Meg said. 'Terrible.'

'Luckily nothing was taken except that strange stone of mine,' Jerrickson reassured them.

But this was far from reassuring to Art. 'You mean the one that seems to change colour when you hold it up to the light? The one you found upstairs?'

'That's the one. It's a strange business. I shall miss it.'

They talked for a while, Art and Meg offering their sympathy, and Jerrickson thanking them and saying everything was all right. 'I need to get the glass in the door replaced, but otherwise there's no real harm done. Except up here,' he said, tapping his head.

'What do you mean?' Art wondered. The stone had been used to focus mental powers – to direct someone's thoughts into other matter. Had it affected Jerrickson?

'Oh, just that I shall be jittery whenever anyone comes into the shop now. I shall worry every time I lock up and go home. It's . . .' He shrugged, unsure what it was. 'It's more than unsettling. To think someone just came in, broke into my property. It's disturbing. The police say it's unlikely they will come back. But, once bitten . . .'

'Did that man come back for his key?' Meg

asked. It seemed an odd question to Art, but she went on, 'The man who came through to the back room yesterday? He saw the stone, though I didn't think he was interested. But he said getting his key copied was urgent.'

Jerrickson frowned. 'How strange,' he said. 'No, he hasn't been back. What with one thing and another, I had quite forgotten about him. But his keys are ready.' He reached under the counter and held up three keys – one old and well worn, the others shining and new.

'Probably nothing,' Meg said quietly. 'I just wondered.'

They walked slowly back to the den.

'You think it's important, don't you?' Meg said.

Art nodded. 'Yes, I do. Oh, I wanted to be sure that old Jerrickson was all right of course. But I needed to be sure that it was *that* stone – Bessemer's stone – that had been taken.'

'But why would anyone want it? And how would they know it was important? That customer who didn't come back – he said getting the key copied was urgent. But I knew he was lying.'

'People do say things are urgent when they're

not,' Art pointed out. 'But it may be worth following up. What was he like?'

Meg sighed. 'Difficult to tell. He was so muffled up and wearing a hat, I can't even be sure it was a man not a woman. Though his voice was deep and sort of husky.'

'Voices can be disguised,' Art said. 'So a boy can sound like a detective,' he added with a grin. 'Or,' he went on thoughtfully, 'to disguise an accent.'

'What do you mean?'

'That stone,' Art said slowly. 'It can affect the mind. Somehow. We know that. Maybe someone – someone with some sort of mental powers – maybe they just sort of *felt* it was there.'

'Someone with mental powers?' Meg stopped abruptly, and turned to face Art. 'Someone like a hypnotist, you mean?'

'That's exactly what I mean.'

'You think this is all connected. The theatre, Edward Watling and now the missing stone.'

'I don't know,' Art admitted. 'But Watling was at the theatre. And for him to behave in the way he did, well, his mind had been affected somehow.'

They were walking again now, almost back at

the den. 'But that all happened before the stone was taken,' Meg pointed out.

'Yes, I thought about that.'

'And?'

'And what if it all went wrong? Whatever he was meant to do, Watling wasn't supposed to blab his secrets over dinner, or to Charlie and us, was he?'

'I suppose not.'

They had reached the side door of the warehouse. It looked as though it was locked, but they had left it so they could open it – the only way into the warehouse.

Art held open the door for Meg. 'So they, whoever *they* are, need to try again. But this time they have to get it right. Now what if they find the stone? Don't ask me how – they can sense it, or they knew about the puppets. Maybe they even worked with them.'

'Spies,' Meg said softly.

Art nodded. 'Our hypnotist friend is Italian, with a distinctive accent, remember. And Italy is a friend of Germany. And Germany . . .'

A squeal of laughter from deep inside the warehouse interrupted Art.

'Flinch and Jonny are back,' Meg said.

'Good,' Art said. 'Then I think it's time we paid another visit to the Castle Theatre.'

Meg nodded. 'I'll meet you there,' she said. 'I'd like to talk to Mr Jerrickson again.' She turned and hurried back towards the door.

'What about?' Art called after her.

'Just a thought.' Meg called back. 'I'll see you there.'

Then she was gone, leaving Art alone with his thoughts and the sound of Flinch's laughter.

By luck more than judgement, Art had timed it so that they got to the Castle Theatre between shows. One audience had departed, and the next had yet to start to arrive. Meg was waiting for them outside, though she offered no explanation of what she had wanted to see Mr Jerrickson about. Art knew better than to ask – she would tell them if and when she wanted to and not before.

'I don't fancy running into that Gregson man again,' Jonny said, eyeing the theatre warily.

Flinch shivered. 'Do we have to go inside?'

'I think we do,' Art said. He had outlined his theory about Giuseppe the hypnotist on their way to Carshalton Street. 'If we can just get a quick look inside his dressing room, we might spot something important.'

'A clue?' Flinch wondered, her eyes wide in anticipation.

'The stone perhaps,' Meg suggested.

'He's not likely to leave it lying around,' Jonny said.

'You never know. After all, he's no reason to suspect anyone thinks it was him who took it,' Art told them. 'From what Meg says he could be the mysterious customer. And the timing fits.'

'He could have slipped out after the performance you watched,' Meg said, 'and been back in time for the next one.'

Jonny nodded. 'He's the last act, so he would have plenty of time before he was on stage again.'

Flinch was nodding too. 'That woman told us he was getting ready for his act. Maybe he wasn't there at all and just told everyone he was busy.'

'Could be,' Art agreed with a smile.

'Still don't fancy meeting our friend Mr Gregson, though,' Jonny mumbled.

'We don't even know if he's here today,' Meg said sternly.

'Then,' Art decided, 'let's find out.'

'How do we do that?' Jonny's face was slightly pale and his voice strained.

'We go and ask to talk to him,' Art said.

The young woman in the ticket booth was more interested in her own fingernails than she was in Art. She inspected them, wiped them on her jacket lapel and rubbed at them diligently with a small metal nail file. Once Art had managed to get her to understand that he did not want a ticket for the next show, she deigned to glance up at him.

After that glance, she returned her attention to her nails. 'So what d'yer want, then?'

'I want to see Mr Gregson,' Art said again. 'The owner of the theatre,' he added, in case she didn't know who he meant.

She shook her head. Or maybe she was just comparing the nails on each hand. 'He don't own the theatre,' she said. 'That Sir Carmichael is who owns it. Mr Gregson, now, he's the manager and you can't see him.' She glanced up again, just for long enough to flash an apologetic smile.

'Why not?'

The woman sighed, put down her nail file and pushed back her unnaturally blonde hair as if to inspect Art all the better. 'You see that notice?' she asked, pointing a near-perfectly nailed finger across the foyer of the theatre.

'Yes.'

Art had seen the poster advertising the fact that the variety show was to be replaced at weekends by performances of *Macbeth*. There was a note to the effect that the first performance was by invitation only.

'Lots of important people are coming to that first night, so everything has to be perfect, doesn't it?'

'Does it?'

'Yes, it does,' the woman insisted. 'So Mr Gregson, he's with the producer this afternoon making the arrangements, isn't he? For the important people. To make sure everything's perfect.'

'Thank you,' Art said, hoping he did not sound too relieved that Mr Gregson was not on the premises. 'I hope everything goes well for it, and that everything's just perfect,' he said as he turned away. 'Why don't you get your nails done for the occasion?'

*

The others were waiting round by the stage door of the theatre for Art to return. Jonny had told Flinch that the stage door was where the performers went in and out of the theatre so as not to have to go through the foyer and the main part of the building. It was a small, very ordinary-looking door at the side of the theatre. It was not even arched like the main doors, and was the least castle-like part of the place that Flinch had yet seen.

She had been fascinated by the stone walls, the huge staircase that rose to the upper floor, the suits of armour standing in alcoves round the foyer. They had passed a large room that Art had told her was the bar – it was full of people and noise. But Flinch had been able to see that the columns that reached up to the ceiling were in the shape of robed women who apparently held the roof up with their hands above their heads.

So the stage door was something of a disappointment. Not many people seemed to use it. She guessed that the performers – the jugglers, singers, musicians, the magician and the hypnotist and everyone – were already inside, waiting for the next show. So she watched carefully as several people approached the door and let themselves in.

'I know that man,' a voice said from behind them. Art was back, and he too was watching the men disappearing through the door.

Flinch knew which man he meant – the fattest and broadest of them had a shock of very red hair. She had seen him before as well, and she struggled to remember where.

'Probably when you went backstage before,' Meg said. 'He'll be a scene shifter or a stagehand or something.'

'What about Gregson?' Jonny wanted to know.

'He's away for the day, sorting out some special performance of a play,' Art revealed, to Jonny's evident relief.

Flinch would have been relieved too. Except she had just remembered where she had seen the red-haired man before. 'He's the one who ate the onion,' she said aloud.

Art was already setting off towards the door. He stopped and turned, his mouth open in astonishment. 'Of course. And those other men . . .'

'We've seen them all before,' Jonny confirmed. 'Well done, Flinch, you're right. That red-haired man ate the onion thinking it was an apple. And the others . . .'

'The others,' Art finished for him, 'were all people who were hypnotised on stage at the show we saw yesterday.'

'But what does that mean?' Flinch asked. 'Why are they here?'

'The same reason Watling was here,' Art said gravely.

Jonny nodded. 'He must be hypnotising them, and ordering them to come back for instructions or something.'

'Giuseppe is still making them do stuff?' Flinch didn't like the sound of that.

'So it would seem,' Meg told her. 'They could be stealing information or anything. Maybe some of them are important people in the government and, like Mr Watling, they're telling him their secrets. We just don't know.'

'No,' Art admitted, 'we don't. So we need to get in there and find out.'

The light faded quickly. Whatever had been done to the rest of the theatre, the cellar and the way down to it seemed to have been rather neglected. The stone steps were worn, the edges crumbling. The whole place smelled musty and damp.

Arthur gave an involuntary gasp as he walked through a huge cobweb. The clammy strands of it stuck to his face and no amount of wiping with his hand seemed to get rid of the feel of them.

'Shhh!' Sarah hissed from behind him. But a moment later she too gave a stifled shriek.

Arthur guessed she had found the remains of the web. 'Watch out for the cobwebs,' he whispered, glad she could not see his smile.

'What now?' she asked, when they reached the bottom of the steps. 'I don't fancy hanging round in this place for long. What if they come to film down here?'

'Just take a look at this spooky cellar, restored to its ghostly glory,' Arthur said in a fair approximation of Kershaw's oily tones. 'Not very likely,' he decided.

But Sarah didn't seem to appreciate his impression. 'What's that?'

'What?' He had no idea where she was

looking. It was so dark now that she could be jumping up and down and pointing, he wouldn't know.

'There's a light. Very faint. Over there.'

Arthur stared into the darkness. She was right, he realised, there was just the faintest glimmer at the far end of the cellar. 'Let's go and see.'

Something touched Arthur's wrist. He almost cried out, but just in time he realised that it was Sarah's hand, reaching for his own. It made sense, he thought, to stay together. He had no idea what state the floor was in, or what might be lying around for them to trip over. Her hand was warm and gripped his own tightly. Surprisingly, he found this reassuring rather than embarrassing.

They made their cautious way towards the light and, as they got closer, Arthur could see that it was a line along the floor. Another few steps and he saw that it was daylight, shining under a door.

Sarah gave an audible sigh of relief and her grip on his hand loosened slightly. 'Emergency exit?'

'Could be,' he agreed. 'Fire regulations or something.'

He had to let go of her hand to feel round the door. He could just make out the rectangular shape in the gloom. His hand touched something cold and rough – rusted metal. 'Push bar to open?' he wondered out loud.

The bar was stiff, and when it gave it moved with a crack that echoed round the cellar. The door swung open a few inches, letting light spill in. Arthur pushed harder, forcing the door over the weeds that were growing up outside it. The door had not been opened for a long time, he guessed.

The door gave out into a small area at the bottom of a flight of moss- and weed-covered steps that led up to ground level.

'I think now,' Arthur said, 'I really do have to get home. But I hope you enjoyed the show.'

CHAPTER FIVE

It was, Art imagined, the lull before the storm. When they had gone backstage at the theatre before, it was immediately after a show. The corridor that ran past the dressing rooms had been all but filled with performers. Now it was almost empty, though there would no doubt be lots of activity as they all geared up for the new show in about twenty minutes.

From the description Mrs Foster, the cleaner, had given, Art had expected the backstage area to look as much like an old castle as the front of house. But from the brief glimpse they had got before Mr Gregson evicted them it was impossible to guess just how far the theme was taken. They had found themselves in a long corridor that ran past the dressing rooms and various storage areas. There was an opening to the general backstage facilities and for the performers to get to the stage itself. The opening was a huge medieval archway with dark canvas curtains across it, though they were pulled aside and tied back now. The walls, ceiling, and even the floor were constructed from huge stone blocks or slabs, and the doors to the rooms looked as if they might have been removed from a cathedral.

There were not nearly as many dressing rooms as there were performers, so Art guessed that some performers were forced to share – probably the band and some of the singers. From the way Mrs Foster had described the theatre to the Invisible Detective, Art knew that at the end of the corridor were Mr Gregson's office and several storerooms before the corridor turned a corner and led to the stairs down to the cellar, where more props and scenery were kept.

'What are we looking for?' Meg hissed.

They were all four standing just inside the stage door, looking along the corridor.

'I did think we'd simply have a wander round and see if we could find anything that seemed relevant,' Art replied. 'But now I think our best option is to find the Great Giuseppe's dressing room. It's obvious he's up to something.'

'But won't he be in there?' Flinch wondered.

'With those people he's hypnotised,' Jonny said.

Art nodded. 'But he'll have to leave to go on

stage, if not before. Which will give us a chance to have a look round.'

'What if we're caught?' Jonny worried.

'Then we just say we're lost, or we were after a signed photo or something.'

Several stagehands appeared from the direction of the main theatre. One of them, a thin, wiry man with a scrawny beard, glared at Art and the others. But he said nothing and they continued on their way.

'We'll attract attention if we just stand around here,' Meg said. 'We should try to find Giuseppe's room. It may not even be on this corridor. Mrs Foster said there were storerooms and rehearsal studios all over the theatre.'

'So where and how do we start?' Jonny asked.

Before Art could answer, the outside door behind them opened and a little grey-haired man came in. He was dressed in the dark uniform of the band, and he was struggling to manhandle a tuba through the door. He stopped and scowled at the children.

'What are you doing? You lost or something?' He sounded annoyed, and Art guessed it had not been easy transporting the tuba.

But before Art could think of a suitable answer, Flinch ran to help the man, lifting up the end of the huge brass instrument.

He blinked in surprise. 'Oh, thanks,' he said. 'Just along here on the right.'

Art, Meg and Jonny stepped aside to let them pass, then followed Flinch, the man and the tuba along the corridor.

'We're looking for Giuseppe, the hypnotist,' Flinch said as she helped.

Not for the first time, Art smiled at her directness and the effect it had.

'Thanks,' the man said again, pushing open a dressing-room door. 'That's a great help. Giuseppe's further down on the same side. It's the door with a silver star on it. We take it down when he's not looking, just to annoy him. But I think he must have a box of them.'

'Aren't you afraid he'll hypnotise you?' Flinch asked in surprise.

The man laughed. 'You're kidding!' He shook his head in amusement, and the door swung shut behind him.

'Well done, Flinch,' Art said. 'This way, then. And let's see if the Great Giuseppe is at home.'

The Great Giuseppe was at home. His door was shut, but the sound of voices was clearly audible from inside.

'Talking to the men he hypnotised, no doubt,' Art said. 'It's a pity we can't hear them.' He pressed his ear carefully to the door, but still all he could make out was the low mumble of voices.

'He's the last act,' Jonny pointed out. 'We might have a long wait till he emerges. Maybe we should come back?'

'Maybe,' Art agreed. 'But we'll give him a few minutes. Just till the performance starts again.'

'We can't wait here,' Meg said. 'He'll see us as soon as he opens the door.'

'He doesn't know who we are, though,' Flinch said.

'No, and that will make him suspicious.'

'Meg's right,' Art agreed. 'He'll expect to know anyone backstage in the theatre by sight even if he doesn't know them by name.'

'So?' Jonny asked.

'So let's carry on to the end of the corridor. I want to see the steps down to the cellar.'

Flinch's eyes widened. 'I don't want to see where the ghost lives.'

'There's no such thing as ghosts,' Meg told her. 'And even if there were, they don't "live".'

The matter was decided for them, however. The door to Giuseppe's dressing room rattled in its frame. The handle turned. The door started to open.

'Quick,' Jonny whispered, and was off.

The door was hinged so that it opened inwards and whoever opened it would have a view of the corridor leading back towards the stage and the outside door. So Jonny, quickly followed by the others, ran in the opposite direction. There was no way Art could keep up with Jonny, but he hoped they would all be round the corner of the corridor before Giuseppe – or whoever came out – looked that way. Or that they would not look at all.

He did not stop to check.

'Who was it?' Jonny asked as soon as they were all safely round the corner of the corridor. There was no sign or sound of anyone following.

'It was the onion man,' Flinch told them. 'He

didn't see us, just went off down the passage the other way.'

Art looked along the corridor. At the far end, he could see the steps leading to the cellar. And, if Mary Foster was to be believed, the ghost. There were several doors between them and the steps and Art listened for a moment at the nearest. Hearing nothing from behind it, he carefully tried the handle.

The door refused to open. But there was a key in the lock – a large, old-fashioned key. Art turned it. The lock clicked and he opened the door. Behind it was a large room packed full of what looked like junk. Clothes and costumes hung on rails; scenery flats – huge boards with stage backdrops painted on them – were stacked against the walls. One was a formal garden framed between two fir trees. Another looked like the inside of a modern drawing room, complete with painted fireplace. Piles of bits and pieces and boxes of props littered the floor. Dirty dustsheets were draped haphazardly over mounds of bric-à-brac.

'We wouldn't find anything in here,' Art decided, 'even if we knew what we were looking for.'

Jonny had pushed the door almost shut behind them and peered out through the gap he had left between the door and its thick wooden frame. 'Can't see anyone,' he whispered. 'I think it's safe to leave.' He turned back towards Art and Meg. And his face went white.

Art was startled by the way Jonny's eyes had widened and the colour had drained from his face. He was looking at something behind Art. As Art turned to see what it was, a thin, ghostly wailing sound made his stomach lurch. He saw Meg beside him, pursing her lips tightly together. And he saw the strange apparition that rose up before them.

The ghostly form was a pale mass that rocked and bobbed about in front of them. You could just about make out the form of arms waving and what might have been a head. As it moved, it wailed like a spirit from hell. It seemed to be gathering itself, as if getting ready to fly across the room at them. Art swallowed – the effect of the inhuman movement and the ghostly wailing held him petrified.

Meg, it seemed, was less impressed. She

walked quickly across to the ghostly figure and tugged the dustsheet off it.

'Stop messing about, Flinch,' she said. 'You're frightening Jonny.'

'I wasn't frightened,' Jonny said for the third time since they left the storeroom.

'Of course you weren't,' Meg said, obviously trying not to smile.

Art knew how he himself had felt, and Jonny was generally more nervous. 'Let's have a quick look further down here,' he said. 'See if we can find any real ghosts.'

There were several more storerooms. Meg stopped outside one, apparently fascinated by the door.

'What is it?' Flinch asked. 'More sheets for the ghosts to use?'

She grinned at Jonny, who stuck his tongue out at her, making them both laugh.

'There's no key,' Meg said.

She tried the door, and it was unlocked. Inside looked very similar to the other storeroom – piles of old props, rows of costumes hanging on rails and scenery stacked against the walls.

'Maybe they've lost it,' Art thought. 'Or Gregson or someone has it for safekeeping or whatever.'

'Then why's the door unlocked?' Jonny wanted to know. 'Anyway, it's all just junk like the other room.'

'Someone's coming!' Flinch hissed at them suddenly.

Art looked back along the corridor, where Flinch was pointing. It was too late to try to hide, the man had already seen them. Best to pretend they were meant to be there. It was the thin, wiry man with the scrawny beard they had seen with other stagehands earlier. He was walking slowly down the corridor towards them, looking thoughtfully at the children.

'If you're looking for Mr Gregson,' Art said loudly, 'then he isn't here.'

'Isn't he?' the man replied. He had stopped a short way from them, his arms folded as he continued to regard them with evident suspicion.

'He's organising the *Macbeth* performance. With the producer,' Art explained.

'I know,' the man told them. 'And he's doing it in his office.' He nodded past Art and the others.

Art turned to look, realising his mistake with a sudden sinking feeling in his stomach. The woman in the ticket booth had not said Gregson wasn't here, Art had just assumed that. And he had been wrong.

As if to prove the point, a door further down the corridor was opening and two people stepped out from the office. One was a man in his thirties with a long, thin face and a rather beaky nose. The other was Mr Gregson.

Gregson stopped and stared at Art and his friends. His face visibly darkened in colour and he spluttered something that resolved itself into an angry cry of, 'You again!'

'Quick!' Jonny called, and ran.

'Stop them, Dexter,' Gregson shouted.

Jonny was fast. But he was not fast enough to get past the wiry stagehand, who moved quickly to block his path. He grabbed Jonny round the waist and all but lifted him off his feet, swinging him round. Art could see Flinch looking for a gap in among the flailing legs and the man holding Jonny – a gap however small she could dive through and escape.

But before Flinch could move, several more

scene shifters and stagehands appeared from behind the man holding Jonny. It was obvious that Art, Meg and Flinch were also trapped.

'I warned you,' Gregson said. His voice was deep with anger and his face was a shade of purple. 'I told you if I ever saw you again you'd regret it.'

Art nodded. 'Yes, sir,' he said quietly, hoping he sounded contrite. 'We, er, we came to apologise. We didn't mean to cause any trouble.'

Gregson stared back at Art, unimpressed. 'If you came here to say sorry, then I'm the Queen of Sheba,' he announced. He smiled thinly at the man standing with him. 'And I'd say that was not the case, wouldn't you, Mr Harris?'

Mr Harris smiled back. His voice was a fawning, nasal whine. 'I'm not sure even my staging skills could convince an audience of that, Mr Gregson,' he agreed.

'The show's due to start in a few minutes, Mr Gregson, sir,' the wiry stagehand said. 'What do you want us to do with these kids?' He pushed Jonny back towards Art, Meg and Flinch. Then he flexed his fingers and bunched them into fists, his knuckles cracking loudly.

Meg pushed in front of Art and looked up at Gregson, her eyes open wide. 'Please don't lock us up in the storeroom,' she pleaded. 'I know that's what you're thinking of doing. But I couldn't stand that.'

Art wondered what she could be thinking. There was no key to the room they were standing outside. But Gregson could hardly miss that. Had Meg seen some way out of the room – some small escape that Flinch could squeeze through so as to let them all out?

'Tell our parents, or get the police or anything,' Meg pleaded. 'Only please don't lock us in that storeroom.'

Gregson's eyes narrowed. He looked at Meg, and then he looked at the door to the room, standing slightly open still. 'All right,' he said to the stagehands. 'Put them inside.'

The men bundled the protesting Meg, together with Art, Jonny and Flinch, into the room and the door slammed shut. Art turned to Meg to ask her what she was up to – or if she was really terrified of being locked in the room.

The door opened again almost immediately.

Gregson stepped inside. 'Very funny,' he said, and held out his hand. 'Give me the key.'

'We haven't got the key,' Jonny said.

'It's missing,' Flinch added.

'We noticed it wasn't there,' Art explained. 'Didn't we, Meg?'

Without saying anything, Meg handed Gregson a large, old-fashioned-looking key. Gregson took it without a word and slammed the door shut again. Art could hear the scrape of the key in the lock.

'You found the key?' Art said. 'Where was it?'

'I didn't find it,' Meg told him. 'It wasn't anywhere.'

'I can't see any way out,' Flinch said in a forlorn tone. She was running round the edge of the room, looking behind the clothes and scenery and props. A pair of small pipes ran across the back wall, carrying water or gas through to the other rooms. But apart from these, the walls were bare stone. 'There's not even a window,' Flinch told them. 'The door's the only way in or out.'

'There's a gap under the door,' Jonny said excitedly. 'Look, it's quite big.'

They all turned to look. 'Even I can't get through there,' Flinch said.

'No, no,' Jonny went on, still excited. 'But we find a piece of paper or even some cloth or thin wooden board or something, and we push it under the door.'

Art could see what Jonny was suggesting. Under different circumstances it would have been funny. 'And then what?' he asked gently.

'And then we push the key out of the lock from this side. There must be a thin stick or some wire or something we can use. The key lands on the board or cloth or whatever, and we can pull it back through.'

Flinch clapped her hands together in delight. 'And we can open the door from the inside. Is that what you were thinking of?' she asked Meg.

'No,' Meg told her. 'Because it won't work.'

Flinch's face fell. 'Why not?'

Jonny was examining the lock, and Art could see that he too had realised the problem.

'It won't work,' Art told Flinch, 'because Mr Gregson didn't leave the key in the lock. He took it with him.'

'So we *are* trapped,' Jonny said. 'Well,

thanks, Meg, for getting us locked in here. Good work.'

Meg tilted her head to one side, folded her arms and looked back at Jonny. There was a hint of a smile on her face. Enough to make Art wonder what she was thinking.

'Where did you get that key?' he asked her again.

'From Mr Jerrickson,' she said. 'It's the key that strange customer brought in to get copies made.'

'The key to this room?' Jonny said quietly.

'Another connection,' Art said. 'The stone must have been stolen by someone from this theatre – they took the key from this room, knowing it wouldn't be missed, as an excuse to get into Mr Jerrickson's shop.'

'Which is all very clever, Meg,' Jonny said. 'But we're still trapped in here, waiting for Gregson and his friends to do goodness knows what to us when the show's over.'

'At least there's no ghosts,' Flinch told Jonny, making his scowl deepen.

But she was wrong.

As they stood and contemplated their fate, as

Meg continued to look at Jonny with a strange half-smile on her face, they all heard the weird, echoing voice.

'What's that?' Jonny asked in an anxious whisper. 'It's not you, Flinch, is it?'

She shook her head.

Art was looking round. 'It's coming from . . .' He walked towards where he thought the sound was coming from, but it got no louder. 'No, it . . . It's coming from everywhere.'

He stood in the middle of the room, looking from side to side, desperate for some clue as to the source of the strange cracked voice that echoed thinly round them.

In the dead silence as they all strained to hear, some of the words were clear enough to make out – a dry cackle of sound.

'By the pricking of my thumbs, something wicked this way comes.'

'Twenty shillings to the pound,' Arthur said. 'And twelve pennies in a shilling. Is that right?'

'You've got it,' Grandad said, satisfied.

'I can't imagine I'll ever need to know that.'

'You'd be surprised. It's good to know about the past. You know what a farthing is?'

'Look,' Arthur protested, 'does it matter?'

Grandad's pale eyes regarded him for a moment as he considered. 'Perhaps not,' he decided. 'But I expect you'll be interested to know how we had to make telephone calls back then. None of your mobile phones, you know. Couldn't even dial directly for most numbers. You'd lift the handset, dial the operator if you weren't connected automatically, and you would need the number and the exchange . . .' He broke off and peered at Art. 'You know what I mean by the exchange?'

For some reason, Grandad seemed to have decided that Arthur needed a crash course in life in the 1930s. Arthur had found it amusing an hour ago. Then it had become rather boring. Now his grandfather's determination to educate him was becoming a little unsettling.

'Maybe I should be teaching you how to use a computer,' he complained. 'That'd be more use.'

Grandad sat back in his little armchair. 'You'd

be surprised,' he said quietly. 'But maybe I have been banging on a bit today. Actually,' he said, changing the subject, 'I did want to ask you a favour.'

'Yes?'

'Can I borrow something from you?'

'Of course. What?' Arthur grinned. 'My computer?'

Grandad smiled back. 'No. You remember that invitation in the casebook – the one to the *Macbeth* performance?'

'You want to borrow that?' Arthur was surprised. 'Well, it's yours anyway, really. You can borrow the whole casebook.'

'No, no. Just the ticket will be ... just the ticket.'

'I'll bring it tomorrow after school.' Arthur glanced at his watch. He ought to be going. Dad would wonder where he had got to. He stood up. 'Why do you want it?' he wondered out loud.

'I promised I would show it to someone.'

'Oh?'

'Yes. I rang round and got in touch with the people organising this show at the Castle Theatre next week. I told them I was at the original *Macbeth* performance, and they were kind enough to invite me along to this one.'

Arthur sat down on the bed again. 'Really?'

'Yes, really.' He seemed pleased with himself. 'Should be quite an occasion. A very nice young man rang me back and wanted to know all about it. I told him I had an original invitation and he was very enthusiastic.'

'He wanted to see it?'

'I told him that if I could bring two guests along, he was welcome to put it on the television.'

Arthur's mouth dropped open. 'You're taking me and Dad?'

'Well, I don't think Shakespeare is really your father's thing, you know. I thought you could bring that young friend of yours from school. Sarah.'

'She's older than me,' Arthur reminded him. 'But yes, she'd enjoy it. In fact . . .' He was going to tell Grandad about their visit to the Castle Theatre the previous day. But then he realised something Grandad had said. 'Hang on. What do you mean, "put it on the television"?'

'They're doing this programme all about the Castle Theatre. Remember, I told you. I think.' He frowned as he tried to remember. 'Anyway, that's who I called, the television people.'

'And who is it who wants to borrow the

invitation and has arranged for us to go to the play?' Arthur asked, but he was afraid he already knew the answer.

'Oh, a very polite young man. You've probably seen him on the telly. Miles Kershaw, his name is.'

CHAPTER SIX

The voice died away into a susurration of whispers. For a while there was silence. Art was still standing in the middle of the cluttered storeroom, trying to make out where the sound had been coming from.

'The ghost!' Flinch said softly.

Meg put an arm round her shoulder. 'It's not a ghost. Just a voice.'

Jonny was as pale as he had been when Flinch dressed up in the sheet. 'Do you think that's what Mary Foster heard?' he asked.

Art nodded. 'I would guess so.'

'I want to go home,' Flinch said quietly. 'Back to the den.'

Art was not sure what to say to this. They were trapped in the small room, with no way out apart from a solid, locked door. And although he wondered if it might just be his imagination, he thought he could hear the whispering of the ghostly voice beginning again. It made him shiver suddenly.

Jonny could hear it too. 'It's coming back,' he said.

'Then it's time we got out of here,' Meg decided. She let go of Flinch and strode purposefully over to the door.

'But how?' Jonny said, his voice a whine of frustration.

'Easy,' Meg told him. 'We use the key.' She held it up for them to see, before inserting it in the lock.

In a moment the door was open and they all but tumbled out into the corridor. Even here, it seemed to Art, he could hear the crackling whisper of the voice.

'Where did you get that key?' Jonny asked in astonishment.

'From Mr Jerrickson,' Meg said, with a self-satisfied smile.

Art guessed she had borrowed the original key and at least one of the duplicates he had made as well. But there was no time for him to tell Jonny this. Down the corridor, towards the steps that led to the cellar, a door was opening – the door to Gregson's office. Art did not waste time trying to sneak away or even duck back into the storeroom. He gave Jonny a shove, grabbed Flinch and pulled her with him, and gathered up

Meg with his other arm, pushing her ahead of him as he ran.

'Come on!' he shouted as they hurled themselves along the corridor, making towards the stage door.

They almost made it.

But as they ran past the dressing rooms, Jonny a few paces in the lead of course, the band emerged from their rooms and blocked the corridor. Jonny skidded to a halt, bumping into a man with a slide trombone. He muttered an apology and tried to push past. There was a double bass in the way now, and Jonny could get no further.

'Hold up,' one of the musicians told them in a loud whisper. 'No hurry. We'll be on soon as we get the nod, then you can rush about in the corridor as much as you like. So long as you keep the noise down.'

Art doubted this was true. He could hear shouts and running feet coming from behind them – Gregson or one of his thuggish stagehands.

'We have to split up,' Meg said.

They did stand a better chance of hiding or slipping away if they were not all together. In any case, Jonny was already tangled in the middle of the musicians, and Flinch seemed to have disappeared entirely.

'All right,' Art said reluctantly. 'Meet back at the den,' he called, hoping Jonny and Flinch would hear. But even if they didn't he was sure that was where they would make for.

'Good luck,' Meg whispered, and pushed her way past a trumpeter. It seemed as though she was heading for the stage.

Art looked round for somewhere to hide. The door to the hypnotist Giuseppe's room slammed shut as he looked at it – no point trying in there. He could hear Gregson's voice clearly behind him now, and he put his head down and shoved his way through the protesting musicians. After a few moments, he seemed to emerge on the other side of the group. But when he looked up he saw that he was actually in the middle of them. There was a long way to go yet, and they would move aside quickly for Gregson. There was a door beside him and, not caring whether there was anyone in the dressing room or not, Art opened it.

He half expected to find Jonny inside, waiting for him. But in fact the room was empty.

There was a small table with a mirror over it and jars and tubs of make-up laid out, a faded armchair, several suitcases piled up in the corner of the small room. The only window set in the stone wall was arched like a castle window. It was slightly open, but it looked far too small for Art to squeeze through.

There was shouting from outside the room now. He could hear Gregson's angry voice above the general sound of the musicians and other performers milling about. 'Check each of the dressing rooms,' the manager was shouting. 'I want those kids found, understand?'

The handle on the inside of the door began to turn. Art ran to the window and threw it fully open. But his first thought had been right – he couldn't even get his shoulders through the narrow gap. If he pushed any further, he realised, he would be wedged there, stuck.

Behind him, the door swung open, and a moment later Gregson stepped into the dressing room.

It made perfect sense to Flinch. They needed to find somewhere to hide and they were interested in investigating the hypnotist Giuseppe. So his dressing room seemed the obvious place to go – they had been standing right outside it. She regretted shutting the door, though. Now she opened it carefully, just the slightest crack – enough to see Gregson standing red-faced with anger outside in the corridor.

She carefully closed the door again and looked round. There was no one else in the room, but it was likely that the hypnotist would return before he went on stage. There was a table just inside the door and on it were the things she remembered he used in his act – including a large onion. She grimaced at the thought of biting into it, like the large red-haired man.

The room was cluttered. The make-up table with its mirror had barely an inch of space on it. Flinch thought about searching the room. But it would take for ever, and she didn't know what she was looking for. Art or Jonny or Meg would know, but they weren't here.

Instead, she picked her way across to the window and opened it, breathing in fresh, onion-free air. It was a narrow window, arching to a point at the top. But Flinch knew she could get out of it if she had to. Leaning forward, she could see that there was a short drop to the ground outside – a narrow path before a wall. It looked as if it led round the back of the theatre to the main road.

Flinch hesitated a moment, then hauled herself up and over the sill. She flexed her shoulders, clicking her arms out of their sockets so they hung limply in front of her. If she wriggled, she could get the rest of her body through before clicking her arms back in and reaching down to the ground. It was all so easy, so natural to Flinch that she found it hard to understand why no one else seemed able to do it. She took her weight on her arms and fell forwards. In a moment she was on her feet, jumping back up at the window so she could push it almost, but not quite, closed. She wanted to be able to see into the room – to watch what Giuseppe did when he returned.

She did not have to wait for long. And when Giuseppe did return, he was not alone. Flinch watched him walk over to the chair in front of the make-up table. Behind him several men followed – the men she had seen arrive at the theatre. The last of them was the enormous man who had eaten the onion at the show.

'Now then . . .' Giuseppe's words carried easily to Flinch outside the open window. But when he spoke, his voice was not his own – it had changed completely from when she had heard him speak before. 'I don't want any mistakes this evening. As soon as the interval is over in a few minutes, you will all take your places as usual. Tonight, this is what I want you to do . . .'

Having seen the calm and organisation of the performance from the auditorium, it amazed Meg how disorderly and confused everything was backstage. She allowed herself to be carried along with the band towards the wings at the side of the stage – and almost got pulled on with them. But she managed to push her way to the edge of the group as they trooped on, relieved to see that the curtain was in any case down.

It was the interval, and stagehands and scene shifters were struggling to get off the stage as the band came on to set up their instruments and music. The next act – dancers and a singer – were already getting themselves prepared in the wings. Meg was jostled and shoved as she stood watching, and she knew she would have to move before someone demanded to know who she was and what she was doing here.

She waited for the last group of stagehands to leave, then joined the back of the group. She could not recall any of them being with Gregson when he had caught them earlier, but she kept her face turned away in case. Which was why she failed to see the man standing in the corridor at the back of the stage. The others all stepped aside, but Meg walked right into him.

'Sorry,' she gasped quickly, and made to move on, not daring to look up at the man's face.

A large, rough hand caught her under the chin, forcing her to stop and look.

It was Gregson, his eyes narrow and his nostrils flaring.

'I don't know how you got out of that store-room,' he snorted, 'but you won't get out of here.'

Meg struggled and kicked desperately, but he wrapped his other arm round her waist and all but lifted her off the ground as he dragged her to the nearest room, opened the door and threw her inside. 'You can stay there until I have time to deal with you properly.'

'What are you going to do?' Meg demanded,

sprawled across the floor. She sounded more confident and assured than she felt.

'Maybe nothing. Maybe I'll get the police and have you arrested for trespassing. Or maybe I'll give you the hiding of your life. We'll see.' Gregson's lip curled in anticipation and he slammed the door shut.

The key scraped noisily in the lock. Meg sat in a depressed heap on the floor and looked round. It was a small dressing room. The only way out was the locked door, and a window so narrow that Meg could tell at a glance she would never be able to squeeze through. But maybe it looked out on to the road. Maybe she could attract someone's attention and call for help.

She pushed the window open as wide as she could, and was met with the sight of a brick wall several feet away. She stared at it so long and so hard that the lines of mortar between the bricks blurred and swam and she realised she was close to tears. She bit back a sob.

Then suddenly a face appeared in front of the bricks – out of focus, large and close up. Startled, Meg gave a shriek of surprise.

'Hello, Meg,' said Flinch.

Once Meg got over the surprise, she helped Flinch climb in through the window. They sat cross-legged on the floor of the dressing room.

'He's not real,' Flinch told Meg. Her face was a picture of disappointment. 'It's all made up.'

'What are you talking about?'

'The hypnotist.'

'The Great Giuseppe?'

'The onion man called him Fred Blinkers,' Flinch said. 'And the hypnotist told him not to use that name. His voice was all different too. I think he's a Cockney.'

Meg was confused. 'The onion man?' she asked.

'No, the hypnotist. Only he isn't.'

Meg sighed. Gregson could be back any moment, and Flinch was spouting nonsense while they just sat and waited. 'What are you talking about?' she asked as patiently as she could.

Flinch sighed. 'He isn't a hypnotist. It's not him. Those people we saw coming in – the ones from the show.'

'The people Art said Giuseppe had hypnotised to obey his orders?'

Flinch nodded. 'They work with him. It's all

pretend. I heard him telling them what he's going to pretend to hypnotise them to do. That man,' she went on, her face a picture of disgust, 'he *likes* eating onions. He ate one while they were there. It stank.'

'You mean those people are part of Giuseppe's act? It's all a set-up?'

Flinch nodded sadly. 'All made up,' she repeated. 'And he isn't even foreign. Like I said, he's a Londoner called Fred.'

Meg nodded. 'Well, I suppose that makes sense. But it means he can't be behind what happened to Mr Watling.'

'Waste of time,' Flinch sulked.

'Not at all,' Meg reassured her. 'Now we know it isn't him, we can look for other suspects.' She glanced nervously at the door. 'Though when Mr Gregson gets back . . .' She left the thought unfinished.

'That's all right,' Flinch said. She put her hand on Meg's shoulder to reassure her. 'You got us out of that other room, so I'll get us out of here.'

Meg looked dubiously at the locked door, then at the narrow window. 'I don't see how.'

Flinch was grinning. 'Easy,' she said.

Arthur spent a long time thinking about what Grandad had said. He took the strange stone he had been given together with the Invisible Detective's casebook from his drawer. Looking at it seemed to focus his thoughts, Arthur had discovered. If you stared at the rounded stone, you could see a cascade of colours swirling in the depths, like crystal held up to the light.

The more he stared into the stone, and the more he thought about things, the more anxious Arthur became. At first, he tried to convince himself that Miles Kershaw wouldn't remember him. He must meet hundreds of people in a week – why should he recall a schoolboy loitering outside a theatre?

But then he realised that Sarah had been with him then as she would be at the theatre. From what Grandad had said, Kershaw was going to welcome them personally, inspect the invitation from 1937 and even do a short interview. He might not remember Arthur. He might not even remember

Sarah. But he would probably remember the two of them together.

And at first Arthur thought that even if Kershaw did remember them, they hadn't actually done anything wrong. It was quite natural under the circumstances that they would have been interested in seeing the theatre. But then he remembered the 'keep your hair on' quip, and he realised that Kershaw might not be terribly pleased to see them. Maybe he would turn them away – could he do that? Certainly he was unlikely to miss the chance of humiliating Arthur by way of getting his own back. On TV. In front of millions of people.

The more he thought about it, the more Arthur realised there was only really one way out of the situation, and even that was not a guaranteed success. He didn't like it, not one bit. But it had to be done.

Sarah was even less impressed with his idea than Arthur had been. She took some persuading, but eventually agreed to return to the Castle Theatre and at least see if Miles Kershaw was there.

'He's probably finished and gone off to do something else by now,' she said. 'I think it's a waste of time anyway. Either he'll remember and is miffed, or he won't and he isn't. I don't see that apologising would do any good.'

Arthur did not like to say that he had been thinking almost of grovelling. If he understood Kershaw, then the man would appreciate a bit of fawning. Better to be contrite in private than humiliated in public. He had put the stone in his pocket that morning and could feel its reassuring weight. It fitted exactly into his palm, and he put his hand in his pocket and closed his fingers round its smooth, warm shape.

Arthur was relieved to find that the grey television van was not parked outside the theatre. The doors were standing open once more, and a man with wispy grey hair was sweeping the floor of the foyer, which now looked finished. It was an impressive area and, standing in the doorway, Arthur felt as if he was really about to enter a medieval castle.

'You want something?' the man asked, pausing to lean on his broom.

'We're looking for Miles Kershaw,' Sarah said before Arthur could reply. 'My friend wants to talk to him,' she added with a sticky-sweet smile at Arthur.

The man with the broom sniffed. 'He's here somewhere,' he announced, making Arthur's stomach lurch worryingly. The man let the broom fall, and the handle bounced and clattered on the stone floor. He shuffled over to the doors into the main theatre, pulled them open enough to stick his head through and shouted, 'Mr Kershaw – someone to see you.'

He did not wait for a reply, but retrieved his broom and carried on with his work. He whistled tunelessly as he did so.

'Having second thoughts?' Sarah murmured to Arthur.

He was, but he didn't want to admit it. He didn't have time to admit it either, as Miles Kershaw appeared through the door, making an entrance and looking round with smile fixed for whoever wanted him. The smile froze as he saw Arthur and Sarah.

'Oh,' he said coldly. 'You again.'

'Er, yes,' Arthur said. 'We umm, well . . .' He wasn't sure how to continue.

But Kershaw interrupted him anyway. 'Look,' he said, 'I'm sorry I snapped at you guys the other day. We were all a bit stressed out and behind schedule. So, anyway – sorry.'

Arthur blinked. He had not expected this. 'That's all right,' he said. 'We wanted to apologise too. For getting in the way.'

Kershaw shrugged. 'No hard feelings, then.' His smile was back in place, and it occurred to Arthur for the first time that it might actually be genuine.

'So how's it all going?' Sarah asked.

'Back on track, thank goodness. Looks like they may actually be ready for the first night on time. Which is a relief, I can tell you. Will you be watching the show on Monday?'

'We'll be here on the actual night,' Arthur told him. 'That's why we wanted to sort of make peace beforehand. You spoke to my grandad and invited us along.'

'Your grandad?' Kershaw frowned, pouted and shook his head. 'Sure it was me?'

'He has an original invitation,' Arthur explained. 'From 1937. Mr Arthur Drake.'

Kershaw's face cleared and he stabbed a finger towards Arthur. 'Of course. He said he wanted to bring a couple of youngsters. Well, I never. That's you, then.' He smiled at them again. 'So who are you?'

'Sarah Bustle,' Sarah said.

'And I'm Arthur Drake.' Seeing Kershaw's confusion, he added, 'Named after my grandad, of course.'

'Of course. Well, nice to meet you both.' He turned to go. But when he got to the door, he paused and turned back. 'You still want to see the theatre?'

'Yes,' Arthur said quickly, not wanting to spoil things by admitting they already had.

'So long as you're quiet, then. They're rehearsing at the moment, but I'm sure no one will mind if you have a quick shufti. Anyone asks, tell them you're with me, right?'

'Right,' Arthur agreed, surprised. But Kershaw had already gone.

The theatre was certainly impressive, and the restoration work had been carried out meticulously. Rather than follow Kershaw through to the main auditorium, Arthur and Sarah went through an archway to the side of the foyer. They found themselves at the bottom of a wide stone staircase that swept up to the circle above. The handrails were polished and carved stone, and a knight in armour stood guard on the landing where the staircase turned back on itself.

At the top of the stairs was an open area with a bar running along one side and seating along the other. The chairs were large and wooden, like those that might be found in a banqueting hall. They were arranged round low tables made from darkly polished wooden planks. Caryatid figures like the one they had seen on the stage stood either side of the arched entrance to the circle seating area. Looking back, Arthur saw that two more held up the pillars that framed the top of the staircase.

Sarah led the way through the bar to the auditorium. They emerged on to a large balcony. Two more caryatids formed the door frame from the inside, and Arthur could see another doorway further along – presumably leading out to another, similar bar or restaurant area. The design seemed to be symmetrical.

The stage was a long way away – and a long way below. The figures standing there were small, but their voices carried easily to where Arthur and Sarah sat themselves down at the front of the gallery and watched the rehearsal.

'*Double, double toil and trouble; fire burn, and cauldron bubble.*'

A man in jeans and a leather jacket was telling the actors and actresses what to do, commenting on the performances, changing his mind about how and where they should move.

'*Fillet of a fenny snake, in the cauldron boil and bake.*'

The performers themselves, disappointingly, were also in normal everyday clothes. It was a scene played out round a huge cauldron. But the three witches wore slacks and T-shirts, and Macbeth might have been on his lunch break from an office somewhere as he waited at the side of the stage. Only the language they used marked them out from anyone else.

'*Finger of birth-strangled babe, ditch-deliver'd by a drab.*'

'You know the play?' Sarah asked.

They had sat themselves in the front row and she was leaning forwards, her chin resting on her hands, which in turn rested on the metal rail that ran along the top of the low wall at the front of the gallery.

'Did it at school,' Arthur said. 'I remember odd bits of it. The general story.'

'Don't tell me whodunit.'

'Don't you . . .' He stopped as he realised she was smiling at him. 'Very funny.'

Below them the witches were dancing round the cauldron, chanting.

'Double, double toil and trouble; fire burn, and cauldron bubble.'

Sarah yawned and twisted round in her seat to look back towards the door they had come through. 'I don't suppose we can get a drink here. I'm thirsty.'

'Cool it with a baboon's blood, then the charm is firm and good.'

'You want to come round and have a Coke or something?' she asked. 'There's some e-mail from the Invisible Detective website, some questions come in that I ought to answer. I could use some . . .' Her voice faded. 'Arthur,' she said, quiet and serious. Her voice trembled slightly. 'Arthur, look!'

But Arthur barely heard. He had taken the stone from his pocket and was staring into its deep inner light. He did not know why. He did not remember doing it. But his whole world was the glow of the stone, and the sound of the words from the stage below.

'By the pricking of my thumbs . . .'

And he felt himself slipping away. Into darkness. There was cold stone beneath his feet and a light flickering somewhere in the gloom. Like a candle.

Sarah reached, without looking, for Arthur's arm, pulling, trying to make him turn. To see what she was looking at: the female figures beside the door, classically beautiful, enigmatically smiling.

As Sarah watched, they trembled and moved and seemed to prepare to step away from the lintel they were holding. Two wooden heads turned, just slightly. Just enough for Sarah to know she was not imagining it. Just enough for the carved, blank, wooden eyes to look directly at her.

'... *something wicked this way comes.*'

CHAPTER SEVEN

Art reckoned he had a lucky escape. He had managed to duck down behind the pile of suitcases just in time. He could hear the door open, footsteps inside the room. Then after a moment, Gregson's gruff voice called out, 'I know you're in here, come on out.'

Art had almost stood up, assuming he had been seen. Almost. Instead he stayed where he was, holding his breath, praying that Gregson was bluffing.

After a few seconds, there came a grunt of annoyance and the door slammed shut. Art counted silently to ten, then carefully peered round the cases. The room was again empty.

Outside, the corridor had also been empty. But Art could hear Gregson's voice coming from towards the stage – blocking his way out. The choice was therefore to stay put or to head back down the corridor towards Gregson's office. And the cellar. Art hesitated only a second before deciding. After all, he had come here at least partly to see the cellar that Mary Foster was sure was haunted. Aside from having heard what might have been the ghost, they had achieved nothing.

He had run quickly and quietly back down the corridor, glancing round several times to check he had not been seen. Luckily, it seemed that the interval was nearly over, and everyone was either in position backstage, ready for the show to start again, or in their dressing rooms preparing.

Now Art stood at the top of the stone steps that led to the cellar below, and he wondered if this was such a good idea. The shadows seemed deeper than he had imagined, the darkness darker . . . And somewhere at the back of his mind he could hear the whispering voice of the ghost. Just imagination, he told himself, and started down the steps.

Each step took Art further into the blackness. Each step brought him deeper into shadow. Each step seemed to amplify the husky, echoing voice, and he could no longer blame his imagination – it was real. It was coming from the darkness ahead of him.

Art paused at the bottom of the stairs. He did not want to go on, afraid of what he might find.

But a part of him felt compelled now to finish what he had started – to discover the truth, however frightening it might be. As he stood, unresolved, the darkness ahead of Art seemed almost solid. But his eyes were adjusting and he could make out the dimmest hint of stone walls, of a curve in the corridor, of a glimmer of light flickering on the other side of the wall. Like a candle or an oil lamp perhaps.

And all the while the whispering, chanting voice seemed to come closer and to draw him on. *'Finger of birth-strangled babe,'* it rasped, and Art took a step forwards, into the darkness . . .

The light was brighter now, evidently a lamp of some sort. Art edged round the wall, peering as he tried to make out what was happening. The cellar opened into a large room, most of it taken up with scenery flats and boxes and baskets of props and costumes. But in the space in the middle of all this, illuminated by the flickering of several candles that guttered and spat as if in a breeze, Art saw –

Nothing.

Blackness.

*

Arthur was plunged into darkness, scrabbling desperately at the stone wall. Instinctively, he knew the door was here somewhere. He could remember how the locking bar felt under his hand – the flaking rust and the cold of the metal. He found it and pushed.

The door clanged open, letting daylight into the cellar from the stairwell outside. The steps were worn and weeds were growing up at their edges. Rubbish had fallen into the space between the bottom step and the door – paper and rotten fruit, even an old paint pot. He jumped over it and ran up the moss-covered steps, gulping in the fresh air and wondering how he had got here, what he was doing . . . Why everything seemed so dull, as if he was looking at it through a layer of grey mist.

The performance was coming to an end. Gregson watched the Great Giuseppe of Naples – or Fred Blinkers of Clapham, as Gregson knew he really was – complete his act. The audience applauded, and the curtain came down.

Gregson sighed. Somehow it seemed to have been a long day. And it was far from over. But before the next performance, he was determined to deal with those blasted kids – or at least the one he had managed to find. He caught hold of a stagehand.

'You found those other children yet?'

'Sorry, Mr Gregson. Reckon they got away in the kerfuffle during the interval.'

Gregson snorted in annoyance and turned away. He would make sure the girl locked in Nancy Milliner's dressing room got enough of a thrashing for all of them. He strode along the corridor, people quickly moving out of his way. He pulled the dressing-room key from his pocket and unlocked the door. He threw it open with a snarl of suppressed rage.

Just in time to see the girl disappearing out of the window. Gregson stood and stared openmouthed. He would never have believed she could get through, but he recognised her coat. And anyway, who else could it be? He ran over and stood looking out of the open window for almost a minute, but the girl had disappeared. He shook his head in disbelief – she must have been terrified out of her wits to squeeze through there, he thought. Which was good. Yes, that would have to do – she wouldn't come back to the Castle Theatre in a hurry, he was sure.

He would have been less certain and satisfied had he turned round sooner. If he had, he might have seen Meg step out from behind the door and slip into the corridor. And he would have noticed that she was not wearing her coat.

Meg ran quickly along the corridor. Now that the show was over, it was almost deserted. Almost – as she ran, a door opened and she cannoned into the figure that emerged.

The breath knocked out of her, Meg collapsed to the floor, gasping. The man she had run into staggered, but remained upright. He reached down to help her to her feet and Meg realized that it was the conjuror – Prester Digitation. He was wearing his top hat, but it had been knocked sideways when they collided.

'I'm sorry,' Meg gasped. She glanced over her shoulder as the magician helped her to her feet. Gregson would not stay long in the dressing room, and if he saw her . . .

'Are you all right, young lady?' the conjuror asked, straightening his hat.

'It was my fault,' Meg told him. 'I'm fine.'
She looked back down the corridor again.

'You were running from someone?' He
sounded concerned, but he was smiling reassuringly. It was, Meg thought, a nice smile. She
remembered Flinch's description of his act, and
her fascination with the rabbit.

'I shouldn't be here,' she told him. 'If Mr
Gregson sees me . . .'

The magician was nodding. 'I quite
understand,' he said. 'Off you go.' He touched the
brim of his hat politely.

Meg glanced back yet again – and saw
Gregson step into the corridor.

The conjuror had seen him too. 'Quickly
now,' he said to Meg. 'I'll keep him busy.' He
stepped round Meg, so that he was between her
and Gregson.

Meg did not wait to find out if Gregson had
seen her. She ran. 'Thanks,' she called over her
shoulder, but she did not look back.

'Why are you wearing Meg's coat?' Jonny asked
Flinch.

He was relieved to see her appear from round

the back of the theatre. She spotted him almost at once and came running over to where he was waiting on the other side of the road.

'I'm helping Meg to escape,' Flinch said proudly.

'By nicking her coat?'

'I never nicked her coat!' Flinch took it off as if to make the point.

'So where is Meg?'

'I climbed out the window so Mr Gregson would think Meg was getting away,' Flinch explained. 'She'll be here soon, once the door's unlocked.'

Jonny nodded, though he didn't really know what she was talking about. No doubt the full story would emerge in time. He hoped that Flinch was right and that Meg would soon appear. He was not disappointed. She came out of the stage door, looked round for a moment, then saw the two of them waiting across the road.

She came running over, taking back her coat from Flinch. 'Thanks,' Meg said. 'It worked a treat.'

'All we need now is Art,' Jonny said.

'Here he is.'

Flinch was pointing to the back of the theatre, the way she had come. Art was there, but he seemed to be standing in a daze. He looked round in obvious confusion, as if not knowing quite where he was. He looked straight at Jonny and the others, but it was as if he had not seen them.

'Art!' Flinch called, waving frantically. 'Over here.'

Art looked back, frowned, then came hesitantly over to them.

'Thank goodness,' Meg said. 'I think we all had a narrow escape there.'

Jonny nodded, and Flinch grinned. 'I helped Meg escape,' she said.

Art said nothing at all. He was still looking round, and Jonny guessed he was worried they might be spotted or followed.

'We'd better get back to the den,' Jonny said.

'The den,' Art said quietly. 'Yes. The den.'

'Are you all right?' Meg asked him. 'Gregson didn't . . . I mean, you weren't caught, were you?'

Art shook his head. 'I don't think so, no.' He seemed unsure for a moment, then, 'Yes,' he decided, 'the den. Jonny's right.' He paused again and looked closely at Jonny. 'It *is* Jonny, isn't it?'

Jonny laughed. 'What are you talking about?' He clapped Art on the shoulder. 'Come on, let's get moving. Last one back's—'

But Meg interrupted. 'No, they're not. We'll all go together.'

'Spoilsport,' Jonny said.

Meg ignored him. 'Did you discover anything?' she asked Art. 'I didn't, but Flinch has some news.'

'About Fred the hypnotist,' Flinch said, beaming.

But Art seemed unimpressed. 'I was in the cellar. I don't know . . .' His voice faded and he shrugged.

On the way, Flinch and Meg explained what Flinch had discovered about the hypnotist and the onion man and his friends.

'Stooges,' Art said.

'What?' Jonny asked

'They're called stooges,' Art explained. 'People planted in the audience to make the trick work. You get it on television too.'

'Television?' Flinch said.

Art frowned. 'But maybe not yet,' he said quietly. 'Forget I said that. Sorry.' He was quiet – unusually quiet – the rest of the way back to the den.

Jonny watched his friend carefully. There was something up, he could tell. He wanted to ask what was wrong, but Meg caught his eye and shook her head. She could see that Art was not himself as well. What had happened to him?

Arthur wanted to tell them, but he didn't know how they would react. Would they help him? He had no idea. In a way he felt he knew them so well, but really he knew them hardly at all. Who could say how they would feel? He wasn't even sure how he felt himself, except confused.

There was an old man in the den. He supposed he should have known at once who it was, but he just felt more bewildered. It was only when Flinch gave a delighted cry of 'Charlie!' that he realised.

'Hello, everyone,' Charlie said. His smile was genuine but tinged with sadness. 'I hope you don't mind me waiting for you in your den. I'm afraid I seem to be making a habit of it.'

144

'Not at all,' Meg said at once. 'Do we, Art?' she added, turning to him.

'Er, no,' he said. 'Of course not. You're always welcome, you know that.'

'Are you taking us to tea?' Flinch wanted to know.

Charlie laughed, but again Arthur could tell that there was an underlying anxiety or worry. 'I'm afraid I have things I must do. But I did hope to catch you here for a moment.'

'How can we help?' Jonny wanted to know. 'What's happened?'

'I was wondering how your inquiries at the Castle Theatre were coming along.'

Meg made a face. 'We've just come from there. Not a lot of progress,' she admitted.

Charlie looked at Arthur for confirmation.

'No,' he said. 'Though there are definitely some odd things happening.' He hoped he wouldn't be asked to elaborate.

'You think there really is a connection between the theatre and what happened to Mr Watling?' Meg asked.

'It seems more and more likely.' Charlie sighed, and ran his hand through his tangled mass of white hair. 'I have to go and see Sir Carmichael Rollason, the owner of the Castle Theatre.'

'I thought Mr Gregson owned it,' Flinch said.

'He's the manager,' Charlie explained. 'Sir Carmichael built the place and owns it. I've known him for years – a lovely man. Without an enemy in the world, which makes it all the more strange and sinister.'

'Why, what's happened?' Arthur asked.

'He was attacked late last night. His house was broken into and he was left for dead. Lucky to be with us still.'

'Burglars!' Flinch declared.

'I would have said so,' Charlie said. 'Except that apparently nothing was taken. So I just wonder if there is some connection to this business.'

'Maybe we should talk to Sir Carmichael,' Meg said.

'He's still unconscious, but when he wakes that might be a good idea,' Charlie agreed. 'Once he is up to visitors. Between us, we may discover what all this is about. That is . . .'

'What?' asked Jonny.

Charlie's eyes were moist as he turned to answer. '*If* he recovers.'

'I should be getting home,' Meg said after Charlie had left them, promising to keep them up to date on Sir Carmichael's condition. She looked at Arthur closely, concerned. 'Are you all right, Art?'

'Yes,' he said, forcing a smile. 'Yes, I'm fine. Just . . . distracted.'

But he knew that Meg could tell he was lying. If he really had been Art he would have realised that before he even answered.

But he wasn't. He was Arthur Drake, all right. Just not *that* Arthur Drake. One moment he had been in the recently renovated Castle Theatre, watching the rehearsals for the opening performance of *Macbeth*. The next, somehow, he was in the cellar under the theatre. And when he found his way out – through the fire door he and Sarah had used before – somehow, everything was different. He was no longer in the London he knew, no longer in his own time. He was Art Drake, the Invisible Detective, in 1937.

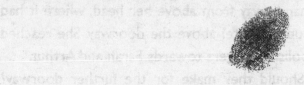

The wooden statues were twisting and trembling, trying to pull themselves free of the structure of the theatre. Sarah did not stop to wonder how or why this was happening. Her first – and only – instinct was to run.

Arthur was sitting staring at something he cradled in the palm of his hand. She did not look to see what it was. She dragged him to his feet and up the stairs. They had to get through the door before the female figures managed to break free. The only other way was over the balcony and down to the auditorium – a drop of maybe ten metres, which Sarah didn't fancy.

'Come on!' she told Arthur. He didn't seem to realise the urgency, didn't seem to see what was happening. He was just looking round in confusion.

'We're in the theatre,' he gasped.

'Of course we are. And we'll be here for evermore if you don't get a move on.'

He frowned, then his eyes widened as he saw the figures. One of the wooden women had dragged her hand away from above her head, where it had held up the lintel above the doorway. She reached out polished fingers towards Sarah and Arthur.

Should they make for the further doorway?

One look was enough to tell Sarah that it would not help. The two figures there were also stirring, waking, moving. It was further to run and she had no idea what was beyond the door. Better the way they knew.

Letting go of Arthur as he stumbled after her, she ran up the steps past the rows of seats. She put her head down and charged through the doorway. A wooden hand grabbed for her – caught her hair, yanking her back.

Arthur cannoned into Sarah's back, pushing her onwards. Her hair was jolted painfully free. She could imagine the statue still holding a handful of it, but she did not look to see. Just kept running.

They raced across the bar, towards the stairs. But the two figures guarding the top of the stairs were also coming to life. With a tearing, wrenching of cracking wood, they hauled themselves away from the bases of their columns and stepped awkwardly and stiffly towards Sarah and Arthur. A jagged length of wood had splintered away from the banisters and remained attached to the hand of one of the women. She raised it, like a lance, and levelled it at them as they skidded to a halt.

'We have to try to dodge past. If we can make

it to the stairs . . .' Sarah glanced at Arthur. He was white-faced, mouth open in astonishment, looking from the walking statues to Sarah and back. 'Are you all right?' she demanded.

'Fine, thank you,' he said, though his voice was shaking. 'Who are you?'

CHAPTER EIGHT

Arthur was not sure what surprised him more – how different everything was or how similar things seemed. Art's dad was very different from his own dad. Or so it seemed at first. Luckily he did not have to spend long with him. Dad was on his way out to work when Arthur got home. They exchanged words in the hall. Arthur did his best to sound upbeat and normal. But he wasn't really sure what 'normal' was for Art. Dad looked at him oddly a couple of times, and Arthur was afraid he would realise his son had been possessed by a child from the future and turn him out of the house. Or worse – the man was a policeman, like his own father, so would he lock him up somewhere in the depths of Scotland Yard?

In the event, Dad left for work without apparently noticing that anything was wrong. Arthur breathed a sigh of relief and went up to his room.

Only when he got there, it wasn't his room. In fact, it was difficult to tell from first glance whether it was Art's room or his father's. Dad was going to be out all night, and Arthur doubted he would sleep much anyway. He would, he decided, have to talk to someone sooner or later. Sooner, probably. There was so much he needed to sort out.

Tomorrow was Saturday, which was a blessing. At least he wouldn't have to find his way to school. What school did he go to? Where was it? What was he supposed to know? He wouldn't even know how shillings and pence worked, he realised, if Grandad – the real Art – hadn't explained it to him. That had seemed odd at the time, but now Arthur thought he understood. Grandad must have known that this would happen. It already had happened to him, after all – whatever it was that had happened to the real Art. And the fact that Grandad was all right and knew gave Arthur hope – it meant that one day, maybe even in just hours or minutes or seconds, everything would return to normal. It had to. But when? And in the meantime, what should he do?

He walked round the house. The basic layout was the same. But everything was different. Like the world outside, it was recognisable, but as soon as he thought he understood it something surprised him and everything seemed to fall apart.

There was no fridge in the kitchen, though there was a light switch and electricity. The cooker was a gas hob, but he had no idea how to light it or what there was that he could – or would be expected to – cook for his tea. He found a packet of biscuits, intrigued by the old-fashioned writing on the wrapper, and the complete lack of ingredient information or a sell-by date. He munched his way through them without tasting a thing.

Before he knew it, the first light of morning was shining into the small living room and he realised he must have fallen asleep. The remains of the biscuits were lying on the carpet close to his feet, crumbs strewn across the floor. There was no vacuum, but a carpet cleaner that you pushed up and down like a broom. It took Arthur a few minutes to work out what to do with it, but the thing seemed to get the crumbs up. He wasn't sure if – or how – he should empty it, so he didn't try. Probably he'd end up with more mess than he started with.

It was odd, he thought, looking round the room. The furniture was obviously old, but it was new. Or at least it looked newer than he would have expected. Like photographs – the older your photograph, the younger you looked in it. Time was a funny thing, like Grandad had said.

He had to start thinking of himself as Art, Arthur decided. It was going to be difficult. But his father had once told him that every problem and difficulty was also an opportunity. And here he was, learning first hand what life was like in the late 1930s. He was actually able to meet Meg and Jonny and Flinch. He had seen photographs of them of course – Grandad had a few – but they were grey and faded and lifeless. They gave no real impression of the characters of Arthur's new friends, just an idea of what they looked like. And still he had been unprepared for the vivid colour of Meg's hair, the intensity of Jonny's gaze, the sheer energy that Flinch seemed to exude even when she was standing still. Despite the photographs and the words in the casebook and Grandad's stories, it was only now, Arthur thought, that he really *believed* in Meg and Jonny and Flinch. Only now that he realised they were real people.

What was more, for the moment at least, Arthur himself *was* the Invisible Detective. And this more than anything brought home to him the truth of his father's comment. He was dreading the Monday night consulting session, frightened almost to death of having to take Art's place in the chair and the coat. But at the same time, he was looking forward to it. As much as he hoped he would be back to himself before the consulting session, he also hoped that he would not, and that he would get the chance to be the great Brandon Lake, just for an hour or two.

It was still early morning when Arthur got to the den. He had been worried he might not find it and wished he had paid more attention to where he was when he started home the night before. But he recognised it easily, and already he felt as if he *belonged* here.

He thought at first that the old warehouse was deserted. He walked slowly round the huge main storage room, examining everything in detail – the ancient, rotting carpets, the brittle wooden supports that held up the gallery that looked about ready to collapse, the windows frosted with dust and grime . . .

'Hello, Art.'

155

The voice startled him and he looked quickly round. Flinch was getting to her feet and yawning. He had forgotten she lived here. It was hardly a home, he thought. But she seemed happy enough and there was nothing much he could do to change things. Better just to accept the way things were and get on with it.

'Hello, Flinch. You sleep well?'

'I always sleep well,' she told him.

Jonny and Meg arrived before much longer. Arthur had spent the time listening to Flinch go over what they had learned so far in their investigations of the Castle Theatre.

'You feeling better today?' Jonny asked.

'We were worried about you,' Meg said. She regarded Arthur warily.

'Are you ill?' Flinch asked, worried.

'No, I'm fine,' he said.

He looked Meg in the eye as he said it. He meant it, he really was fine now. Thinking things through had convinced him that everything would be all right. Eventually. It would be hard, it would be strange, but it was OK. Meg could see he was telling her the truth, and she seemed to relax slightly.

'So what should we do?' she wondered.

They were all looking at Arthur – or rather, as they saw it, they were looking at Art – expecting him to have a plan.

'I suggest,' he said, 'that we call on Charlie and see if there's any news on the condition of poor Sir Carmichael.'

Charlie was in far better spirits, Meg thought, and he insisted that the children go with him to visit his old friend. Sir Carmichael was now recovering well, he told them with some pride: 'Doctor says his skull must be made of cast iron. He's as tough as an old boot, is Carmichael.'

Weathers drove them all over to Sir Carmichael's large town house. Despite the attack, Sir Carmichael had refused to be taken into hospital and was now confined to bed. They waited outside on the landing while Charlie went in to see him first. He emerged a few minutes later, smiling with relief.

'You can tell he's on the mend,' Charlie said. 'Sent me on an errand to the theatre to ask Mr Gregson how the rehearsals are going.' He shook his head. 'Chap thinks he's still giving orders in the army, I tell you.'

'Is that the rehearsals for *Macbeth*?' Arthur asked.

Charlie frowned. 'What do you know about that?'

Arthur shrugged and looked confused.

'They told Art about it,' Flinch said, and Arthur seemed relieved at the explanation.

'Did they tell you why it's special?' Charlie wondered.

They all shook their heads.

'Then neither shall I,' he said, with a sly grin. 'Not yet anyway. But there is indeed a special first-night performance tomorrow and, not surprisingly, Sir Carmichael is keen to know that the preparations are proceeding according to plan. Don't wear him out with your stories and questions,' he warned them, looking hard at Flinch. 'And I'll be back before you know it.'

Sir Carmichael was propped up in bed, waiting for them. He was smaller than Meg had expected, a slight man with a wide smile and pale eyes. His head was wrapped tightly in a bandage, but tufts of grey hair poked out from underneath. His room was immaculately tidy, and when Meg noticed a display case attached to the wall that held several medals she remembered that Charlie had said he was in the army.

'Welcome, welcome,' Sir Carmichael said as soon as they entered the room. He struggled to sit up more. 'Sorry you have to find me laid up like this on me sickbed, but the dratted doctor won't let me up for a while yet. So,' he went on, looking at each of them in turn, 'Charlie tells me you're associates of the famous Invisible Detective. That a fact?'

They all nodded solemnly.

Sir Carmichael smiled thinly. 'Quiet associates, it seems.'

'Oh, no,' Flinch said at once. 'We do lots of talking.'

'That's good,' Sir Carmichael told her kindly. 'Because I can't do much more than talk at the moment. Damned fellow cracked me on the head with a blunt instrument so hard I saw explosions the like of which I've not seen since the war. I tried reading the paper this morning, but it's all still a bit blurred, I'm afraid. I hope the chap comes back,' he added. 'Give him a taste of his own medicine if he does, I can promise you that.'

As he spoke he produced a poker from under the sheets and waved it violently in the air.

Flinch gave a startled shriek, and they all took a step back.

'Oh,' Sir Carmichael said. 'Sorry.' He cleared his throat and stuffed the poker back under the bedclothes. 'Now, then,' he decided, as he settled himself down again. 'What shall we talk about, eh? I gather you're interested in me theatre, what?'

'That's right, sir,' Arthur said.

He seemed more deferential than usual, Meg thought. Perhaps the poker had unsettled him. Or perhaps his experiences in the cellar of the theatre had upset him more than he was letting on. He just didn't seem himself today.

'Why's it look like a castle?' Flinch asked. 'I like it, but why?'

'Ah!' Sir Carmichael held up his finger as if awarding points for good questions. 'Yes, excellent notion that. Capital. Spot on.' He nodded several times before continuing. 'When I was in France, back in '17, my unit was sent to secure a little French village called Château.'

'That means castle,' Arthur said.

Sir Carmichael nodded again. 'Does indeed. Top marks, my lad. In fact that's about all there was there. A few houses. Odd farm. And this dirty great castle. Not that old, mind you. More Gothic than medieval, if you catch my drift. Anyway, the Bosch . . .' He paused. 'That was the enemy, the Germans, you know,' he explained. 'Anyway, they had taken this castle and were using it as a base. We were told there were hundreds of them there, but in fact it was just half a dozen together with the chappie who owned the place. Built it too, clever chap. As I say, it wasn't really very old.'

'Did you win?' Jonny asked.

Sir Carmichael seemed to straighten in the bed. 'We did indeed, young fellow-me-lad. We did indeed. Dashed pity, though. Not knowing how easy it would be, we bombarded the castle for a whole morning before we attacked. Probably could have just walked in and taken it straight away. As it was, the place was in a pretty bad state before we realised there wasn't a whole army in there after all.'

'So you named your theatre after it,' Meg said.

'More than that. When the war was over, the following year, I went back. The castle was the only thing there for the villagers. Provided employment and owned the farmland. Without it they were in a bit of a state, I can tell you. So I bought it from them. Not the land, you understand, just the structure, the fabric if you will. And I had anything that wasn't too damaged dismantled and shipped over. Used it as materials to build and furnish my theatre. Panelling, statues, even roof tiles. The lot. And now it's the Castle Theatre, named after Château Château – Castle Castle in English, I suppose.'

'It's very impressive,' Meg assured him.

'Thank you.' He stared off into the distance, and Meg realised he was looking at the medals in the case on the wall. 'I hope it did the villagers some good too.'

On the way to the Castle Theatre, Charlie had written down as many of Sir Carmichael's questions as he could remember. He was certain he had forgotten several, but he hoped to glean enough information to keep the man happy. The performance that mattered was tomorrow night, and Charlie too was determined that all should go well.

It certainly seemed as if Gregson and his producer, Harris, had things well in hand. Rehearsals took place every evening those last few days, replacing the second evening performance of the variety show. All of Sunday was set aside for dress rehearsals ready for the evening. Charlie was left in no doubt that Gregson and the others appreciated the importance of what they were doing, and he imagined the additional strain and stress went some way to explaining Gregson's intolerance to the Cannoniers. But Charlie did not mention the children to him; better to keep the man focused on the job in hand.

All the same, he admitted to himself, it was a worry that it seemed the Castle Theatre might somehow be connected with the strange behaviour and bizarre death of Edward Watling. Charlie was pondering whether this in itself should be enough for him to recommend a postponement of the performance as he left the theatre. He was making his way back along the long corridor that led from Gregson's office, out past the dressing rooms, when he heard someone call his name.

'Lord Fotherington!'

Charlie turned and saw that a tall, thin man was hastening along the corridor after him. He had not been there a moment ago, so Charlie assumed he had come out of one of the dressing rooms. He certainly looked the theatrical type – dressed in morning suit and wearing a top hat. He carried a short stick, or perhaps, Charlie realised, it was a wand. Black with white tips at each end.

'Can I help you?' Charlie asked.

The man was out of breath, red-faced and perspiring. He seemed nervous, lifting his hat to wipe his brow with a grubby handkerchief. 'I am so glad I caught you,' he said in a serious tone. 'There is something I have to tell you. About tomorrow . . .' He paused and looked all round, as if afraid they might be overheard.

'About the performance?' Charlie prompted. 'About *Macbeth*?'

'Please,' the man said urgently. 'It is bad luck to mention that name without good cause. Especially here in a theatre.'

'You are superstitious.'

'Perhaps,' the man admitted. 'But that is not why . . . Please,' he said again, 'a moment of your time? In private? It will be well worth your while, I promise you.' He swallowed nervously and again wiped his damp brow.

'Of course,' Charlie said. 'If it is important. Though I am in rather a hurry, I'm afraid.' Better to leave himself an excuse to get away if it turned out to be more nonsense about quoting *Macbeth* being unlucky or some such.

'Thank you, sir.' The man was evidently relieved. 'I am so sorry,' he said as he led the way back down the corridor. 'My name is John Prester. I'm the conjuror in the variety show. My stage name is Prester Digitation – rather good, don't you think?'

Charlie did not say what he thought. The man was nervous, looking round furtively the whole time as if afraid they might be seen together.

'Just along here,' he whispered to Charlie as they passed the closed door of Gregson's office. 'There's something I have to show you.'

They continued along the corridor. Towards the steps down to the cellar.

*

'What happened to the owner?' Arthur asked. 'You said he was in the château when it was bombarded.'

'Yes,' Jonny said. 'What did he do with the money?'

'Did he build another castle?' Flinch wanted to know.

Meg smiled at the thought.

'Don't know, to be honest,' Sir Carmichael told them. 'But the original owner, the man who built the chateau, got none of the money, I'm sorry to say. He was killed in the bombardment. Most tragic.'

'That's sad,' Flinch said quietly.

'So who did you buy it from?' Meg asked.

'He had children. They inherited, and I bought what was left from his son.' Sir Carmichael smiled. 'Odd chap, I gather, though I never met him myself. All went through lawyers and so on, you know. Yes,' he continued, 'I gather there was some bitterness.'

'About the death of the father?' Arthur asked.

'And the destruction of the family home. Understandable, of course. Regrettable.' Sir Carmichael sighed. 'Well, *I* regret it. But can't be helped now.'

'What happened to the son?' Meg asked, as much to break Sir Carmichael out of his melancholy as because she wanted to know.

'Joined the theatre, I understand.' Sir Carmichael smiled at the thought. 'Up until 1919, anyway. Apparently he had some sort of conjuring act.'

Sarah just stared at Art.

'What do you mean, who am I?'

He shrugged, shook his head, glanced fearfully at the approaching statues. 'I know this is the Castle Theatre, but how did I get here?'

'This really isn't the time . . .' Sarah said. She grabbed him by the shoulders. 'We have to get past them before . . .'

The splintering of wood from behind told her it might already be too late. The caryatids behind them were also free now. She pushed Art forwards, towards the stairs.

'Why am I dressed like this?' he said as he stumbled onwards. 'What's going on? *Who are you?*'

She ignored him, tuned him out. Time to worry about Arthur's fit or whatever he was having later. 'Table,' she snapped.

To his credit, even in his current state he realised at once what she meant. 'Good idea.'

The low bar table was much heavier than it looked. The wood was rough and gnarled. Sarah took the front, Art lifted the back. They held it by their sides, braced, like a battering ram.

'Come on, then!' Sarah cried. 'The one on the left.'

They stumbled at first, not used to the weight. The table made running awkward, banging into their sides. Sarah grazed her ankle on the bracing strut between the table legs. But gradually they got in step, into the rhythm, and increased their speed.

By the time they reached the statue, they were running full tilt. The table slammed into the caryatid, catching it right in the stomach. Sarah expected it to double over in pain, but it was made of wood. It felt nothing. The impact slammed it backwards, knocking the creature off its feet and sending it flying. It crashed into the side of the bar, still without changing position — stiff and upright. Like a wooden statue. The table was wrenched from their grip by the thudding blow. Sarah felt the vibrations run painfully up her arms as she continued to run.

She did not wait to see how quickly the thing

recovered. She was sure it would simply get up and follow them. The second of the statues from the stairs was already turning after them. The two from the gallery could not be far behind.

But they were past them now. Starting down the stairs. Safe.

Except that even the stairs seemed to be alive. The banisters were shaking under Sarah's hand. With a rasping scrape of sound, one of the steps seemed to slide away from under her feet. She cried out, almost fell, grabbed for Art. He caught her by the arm and pulled her over the stair that was already crumbling and falling away. Together they leaped down the last few steps and arrived in a rolling, bruised tangle on the landing.

Art was on his feet again first, pulling Sarah up after him. She smiled her thanks, and they turned to run down the final flight of steps. But their way was blocked.

The empty suit of armour was standing in front of them. Stiff and clanking, it raised its sword.

CHAPTER NINE

If he realised what impact his words had had on the children, Sir Carmichael did not show it. They were quiet for a while, and Jonny could see that the others too were thinking through the implications of what they had learned.

Sir Carmichael gave a sudden, enormous yawn and admitted he was tired. 'You're welcome to stay here until Charlie gets back,' he told them. 'It's been nice to have some company. Someone to talk to and all that. I'll have Beryl bring some tea to the drawing room while I get some shut-eye.'

Beryl was the maid, summoned by a bell-pull beside the bed. She curtsied and nodded and said 'Yes, sir' a lot, before leading the children downstairs to the drawing room and promising to return soon with tea and – prompted by Flinch – cake.

'So it's the magician, not the hypnotist, we should have been investigating,' Jonny said as soon as they were alone.

'So it seems,' Arthur agreed.

He sounded more himself now, Jonny

thought. But he was still worried at how quiet and nervous Art seemed – it was so out of character.

'I can't believe that's right,' Meg said. 'He seemed so nice and friendly. He helped me escape from Gregson.'

'He didn't know we suspected him,' Jonny pointed out.

'We didn't, not then,' Arthur said.

'He does clever tricks, though,' Jonny went on. 'More impressive than the hypnotist, Fred whatever-his-name-is.'

'It's only more impressive because now we know how the hypnotism is done,' Arthur said. 'If we knew how the conjuror did his tricks they'd not be so impressive then.'

'I suppose not.'

'I like his rabbit,' Flinch said. 'And the lady seemed nice. The one he cut in half.'

'We don't know that the conjuror is behind what's going on,' Meg said. 'We're just guessing.'

'That is true,' Arthur agreed. 'But he would seem to be our prime suspect now.'

Flinch frowned. 'Our what?'

Arthur went slightly pink, which amused – and surprised – Jonny. 'I mean, he's the most likely person to be responsible for everything. Given what we know. But Meg's right,' he went on quickly. 'We don't have any proof. There's nothing to say he's the son of the man who built the castle out for revenge on Sir Carmichael for killing his father and destroying then taking the castle.'

'He paid for it,' Jonny said. 'But that could be what's going on.'

'How do we find out?' Meg asked.

Flinch was still frowning. 'If he's a bad man and we catch him,' she said slowly, 'who will look after the rabbit?'

Arthur grinned. It was the first time that Jonny could remember seeing him smile since they had escaped from the theatre the previous day. 'I expect his assistant would look after the rabbit,' he said. Then, more seriously, he continued, 'But there must be more to it than just revenge on Sir Carmichael. How is it connected to what happened to Edward Watling and the secrets and everything? When we thought it was the hypnotist behind it all, it was obvious what was happening.'

That surprised Jonny. 'Was it?'

'Wasn't it?' Arthur said, confused. 'I mean, I assumed that the hypnotist was mesmerising people in government or whatever, and using some trigger phrase to get them to perform a predetermined act of some sort. So they're primed to recite secret papers or jump out of a window or something when they hear a particular phrase in the right tone of voice or something. Like in that film . . .' He broke off, shrugged and looked away. 'Just a thought.'

Jonny couldn't think what film Art was talking about. They occasionally went to the pictures, but he didn't know Art had been to any films he hadn't seen himself. Perhaps he was thinking of a book, or misremembering. But what Art had said seemed to make sense. Except now they knew that the hypnotist was innocent.

'Perhaps,' Meg said, 'the conjuror does hypnotism too.'

'Then why not use it in his act?' Jonny wondered. 'Though he does guess cards and that number and stuff.'

'Because there's another hypnotism act already,' Meg said. 'He wouldn't want to copy.'

'And he wouldn't want to draw attention to

his powers by using them on stage while he's out hypnotising people in real life,' Arthur added.

'But why is he doing it at all?' Flinch wondered.

Arthur looked uncomfortable at this. 'Well,' he said slowly, 'maybe another country wants to get control of our politicians and leaders, so they make particular decisions. They want our secrets too, that's obvious. But then, when the war comes . . .' Again, he stopped short, as if he thought he had said too much.

'You think we really will go to war with Germany?' Jonny asked.

'Not for a while,' Arthur said. 'And maybe the idea is to stop us declaring war by accepting whatever happens, whatever Hitler does.' He was getting frustrated and waved his hand as if to dismiss the subject. 'I don't know.'

At that moment, Beryl brought in a tray of tea things, and they were silent for a while as she poured the tea and cut the cake. She had brought an extra plate and cup for Charlie when he returned.

When Beryl had left, telling them to ring if they needed anything else, Meg said, 'So how do we find out if the conjuror practises hypnotism and if so what he's doing?'

Before anyone could answer this, the door opened.

It was Charlie. He came and sat down next to Flinch. 'Ah, tea. Good,' he said, with a smile.

'Everything all right at the theatre?' Jonny asked.

'Everything is absolutely fine,' Charlie said, in a measured, almost expressionless tone. 'There is nothing to worry about. Nothing at all.'

'Rehearsals going well, then? Arthur asked.

'There is nothing to worry about,' Charlie said again. His face was as expressionless as his voice. 'Nothing at all.'

'That's a relief,' Jonny said. 'Though we are a bit worried about the conjuror.' He glanced at Art and Meg to check they were happy to tell Charlie what they had discovered.

'The conjuror?' Charlie said, smiling now. 'Oh, he's not a bad sort. His real name is John Prester, you know. We exchanged a few words after I'd checked up on *Macbeth* with Gregson. Seems a nice enough chap. More cake, Flinch?'

'What is *Macbeth*?' Flinch asked.

'It's a play by William Shakespeare,' Arthur told her. 'About witches and a man who usurps the throne of Scotland.'

'Who what?'

'He kills the king and takes over in his place,' Charlie said.

'There's a ghost in it too,' Arthur said quietly.

But before Jonny could pick up on the thought, Charlie was talking again. 'And tomorrow evening,' he said, 'there is a special performance of the play at the Castle Theatre to mark the fifteenth anniversary of the opening of the theatre in 1922. Sir Carmichael is very proud.'

'So what's special about it?' Flinch asked through a mouthful of cake.

'Oh, I can't tell you that,' Charlie said. 'It's all very hush-hush, you know. But lots of very important people are coming.' He leaned forward and continued in a low voice, 'Including the Prime Minister and several of the Cabinet.'

Arthur was looking at Jonny as he said, 'Is that safe, do you think? I mean, having all those important people together in one place at the same time?'

Charlie's smile faded and his face became

blank. 'Everything is absolutely fine,' he said, in exactly the same tone as he had used before. 'There is nothing to worry about. Nothing at all.'

Arthur nodded grimly. 'So you said. By the way,' he went on, 'what did you talk about with the conjuror?'

Charlie's face faded into a frown. 'You know,' he said in a puzzled tone, 'now I come to think about it, I have no idea. I remember he said he wanted a quick word about something. Something urgent. And then . . .' He sighed. 'Well, it can't have been important, can it?'

Jonny and Arthur exchanged glances. Meg too was watching Charlie carefully as he helped himself to more cake.

'No,' Jonny said to himself. 'No, it can't have been important.'

It was late afternoon by the time they got back to the den. Flinch was not used to Art being so quiet – he had said hardly a word the whole way from Sir Carmichael's.

They settled themselves on the huge, dusty rolls of carpet in the main area of the old warehouse. Jonny and Meg had been teasing each other all the way back. Jonny was saying how he thought the magician was handsome and didn't Meg agree. Meg was telling Jonny he was just jealous because he didn't know how the tricks were done. But there was a nervousness and unrest beneath their amusement and laughter. Flinch could tell that they were avoiding saying what they really thought.

So as soon as they were all sitting round, Flinch said, 'What's wrong with Charlie?'

'You think there's something wrong with him?' Meg asked.

'Don't you? He just kept saying the same things.'

Meg sighed. 'I thought it was just my imagination. I hoped it was.'

'I think we all noticed,' Arthur said. 'He was fine, and then whenever we mentioned this *Macbeth* performance he sort of . . . changed.'

'Like he didn't want to talk about it,' Jonny said. 'Though he told us more about what's going on tomorrow night than he did before.'

Arthur was nodding. 'Yes, that's odd too, isn't it?'

'He really didn't seem himself,' Meg said.

Arthur made a sound that might have been a laugh or a cough or a snort, Flinch could not tell which. 'Is he all right?' she asked. She liked Charlie. She hoped he wasn't ill or anything.

'I'm sure he is,' Arthur told her. 'Only . . .'

'Only he's dead set on this performance going ahead,' Meg said.

'And now he seems to recite the same words in the same way whenever anyone asks about it,' Arthur pointed out.

'And he has seen the conjuror,' Jonny added.

'What does that mean?' Flinch wanted to know.

'It means I think we're in trouble,' Arthur said quietly.

He had seemed odd the last day, Flinch thought. But now, as he leaned forward and told them what he thought, counting off the points as he made them on his fingers, Flinch was sure that the old Art was back.

'Let's go over what we know,' Arthur said. 'Edward Watling was hypnotised or something, so that he would perform some specific act when given a particular stimulus. So someone phones him and says a special phrase and he goes to the Castle Theatre for more instructions, or he jumps out of his office window. Or he recites secret information on cue.'

'And you think Charlie has had the same treatment?' Jonny asked.

'I do. Not so extreme, maybe done very quickly.'

'By the conjuror at the theatre when they met?' Meg asked.

'And that's why Charlie can't remember what they talked about. He's been hypnotised into forgetting it, and to say that there's no problem and the *Macbeth* play must go ahead no matter what.' Arthur looked round at them. 'The question is, why? We are pretty sure that the conjuror is mesmerising people – important people. He's instilling some key phrase or trigger in them to make them do things when prompted. He might be using that strange pebble he stole to somehow amplify that effect.'

'Because it went wrong with Mr Watling,' Flinch said. She thought she understood what Art was saying.

Jonny was sitting with his mouth open in

realisation. 'The performance,' he said. 'You think that the conjuror is somehow going to hypnotise the people who come to see *Macbeth*. Maybe catch them during the interval or something?'

'The Prime Minister,' Meg gasped. 'And all those people. Surely he'd never be allowed to see them alone?'

'We have to find out how he's planning to do it, then,' Arthur said.

Flinch looked from Meg to Arthur. 'But why is he doing it?'

'To get secrets. To make sure that if Hitler invades Poland . . .' Arthur paused, blinked and added quickly, 'for example, then we won't declare war on him but come to some agreement. A signature on a piece of paper as appeasement. There are loads of possibilities.'

'All those people, doing things they aren't meant to,' Flinch thought out loud. 'That's . . .' She struggled to think of a word to describe how she felt. 'That's *wicked*,' she said.

Arthur smiled grimly. '*By the pricking of my thumbs, something wicked this way comes*.'

'What?' Meg said with a frown. 'What are you talking about?'

'It's a line from *Macbeth*,' Arthur said.

But Flinch had recognised the words and she knew what else it was. 'It's what the ghost says. In the theatre, when we heard it.'

'It said that?' Arthur demanded, on his feet suddenly.

'You were there,' Meg told him. 'We all heard it. Flinch is right. I'd forgotten, but she's right.'

'Then that's it,' Arthur said. 'Maybe it's even the trigger phrase. I don't know how the ghost comes into this, but it can't be a coincidence.'

'He doesn't need to see them alone,' Jonny said. 'If he's going to plant this phrase or whatever in their minds. Don't you see?' he said, looking round at them all. 'It's a line from the play. I bet all the phrases and keys or whatever he uses come from *Macbeth*. He's going to do it during the actual play.'

Arthur was nodding in agreement. 'Somehow he's planning to hypnotise the whole audience.'

'Then,' said Meg simply, 'we've got to stop him.'

Art's mind was in a whirl. He had been given no time to work out what had happened. One moment he was down in the cellar, the next he was up in the gallery, with a girl he had never seen before who was wearing trousers and behaving very strangely. Not as strangely, he had to admit, as the whole fabric of the theatre building, which seemed to be coming to life around them.

And now he was faced with a knight in armour, though he suspected that if he was able to look inside he would find the armour was actually empty. The good thing, he supposed, was that it saved him from having to worry about where he was and what had happened to him.

Instead he focused on the immediate problem. The knight took a scraping step forwards, the sword chopping towards them. Art pushed the girl to one side, drawing the knight after himself the other way.

'Down the banister, quick!' he told her.

She tilted her head to one side, just like Meg

did when she was not sure about something. 'You *are* joking,' she said.

'No,' he told her. 'I'm not joking.'

The sword sliced so close to him he felt the air move with it.

'All right, then.'

She sounded almost grudging. But instead of sliding down the banister as he had expected, she hurled herself at the suit of armour. Her shoulder cracked into it and the knight was knocked sideways. The head – or rather the helmet – toppled off as it staggered.

The girl had managed to push past the headless knight and she half ran down the stairs, half slid down the polished stone banister – leaning over it on her stomach, her feet delivering a final kick at the knight.

The armour crashed to the floor as Art leaped after the girl, following her example and sliding after her. He did not look to see what the knight was doing. As soon as he reached the bottom of the stairs, he was on his feet, running after the girl – through the foyer.

The huge main doors of the theatre were swinging shut, apparently of their own accord. The girl leaped through and Art was close behind. He sprawled across the pavement as the doors slammed shut behind him.

The girl had managed to stay on her feet. She helped him get up. 'You're really not yourself, are you?' she said.

'No, I'm not.' He was looking round in confusion and astonishment.

'And you really don't know who I am?'

He shook his head. Everything was different: the buildings had changed or gone, the road surface, the street lights, even the smell of the air . . .

'I'm Sarah,' she said. 'And I'm wondering what the heck's going on.'

It had been an effort to get him to talk. But as they stood outside the theatre, eventually, hesitantly, expecting her not to believe him, Arthur – or rather Art – told Sarah who he thought he was.

'I don't know what to believe,' she confessed. 'But having been chased by wooden statues and an empty suit of armour, I'm open to just about anything weird right now.'

Her first instinct was to get help, to find someone and tell them the theatre was coming to life and trying to kill them. But outside, in the dying light, that sounded just too bizarre for words. And when they cautiously tried the theatre doors, they swung open easily. Inside, everything seemed normal. If she had been alone she would have thought she had imagined it. The suit of armour was back in place on the landing. The staircase seemed to be intact.

'I'm not going up to check,' Art told her, 'but I'm willing to bet those wooden statues are back in place, with barely a scratch to show they ever moved at all.'

'So what do we do now?'

'I haven't a clue,' he confessed, leading the way outside again. 'I don't know where we are or what's going on, really. But,' he said with evident sincerity, 'thank you.'

'That's OK,' she told him with a smile. 'We have to get you and Arthur – my Arthur – swapped back somehow. I know someone who might be able to help.'

'Before that,' he said, 'I need some advice.'

'Oh?'

'Not from you. No offence meant. But I want to go to Jursall Street.'

'To the haunted house?'

He was surprised. 'You know about that?'

'I know lots of things,' she told him.

How much he understood of what she told him about herself and Arthur, Sarah had no way of telling. Art was distracted to say the least. He was constantly surprised by what they saw. The most normal things – cars, pedestrian crossings, an aeroplane high above them almost in the clouds, the colour of the street lights as they flickered on, neon signs – they all held his attention.

It seemed to take for ever to get to Jursall Street. They caught a bus, and that at least seemed to be familiar to Art, though he did ask her where the conductor was and insisted on examining the coins she had left after paying.

She waited outside the house as he went in. He had been rather coy about what he was up to, but she knew from Arthur that the house was somewhere that seemed to be fixed in both their times – the present and the 1930s. It was somewhere that Arthur had claimed he could bridge the years and communicate with Art, using the strange clock he had showed her when they were in Cornwall. It seemed a long time ago.

Whether it would work now that Art was actually here in the present with her somehow, she didn't know. But she had a simpler and more straightforward way for Art to find out what had happened in the past. She would take him to see his grandfather.

Or rather, Arthur's grandfather.

Which meant – if this really was Art – that he would be meeting himself.

CHAPTER TEN

Without Charlie's help, they could none of them think of a way to stop the performance from going ahead. The best suggestion was to appeal to Sir Carmichael directly. But, as Jonny pointed out, he was likely to defer to Charlie. There was no doubt that Sir Carmichael wanted the performance to go ahead, whether he was well enough himself to attend or not.

In fact, Arthur thought as he made his way home, given Sir Carmichael's headstrong character, he was less likely to postpone or cancel the performance now than he would have been before he was attacked. If they suggested that the fact someone had tried to kill him had anything to do with the proposed performance, he would be adamant it must go ahead, and confound them. Had the conjuror, or whoever it was, intended to incapacitate Sir Carmichael so that no one was able or willing to call off the play?

Or perhaps the hatred of the son of the original castle owner was simply getting the better of him. He couldn't wait until the performance but had to deal with Sir Carmichael ahead of time.

The more he thought about it, the more Arthur decided this must be the case. No one could know how he would react to the attack, but for the hypnosis plan to work all must seem perfectly normal when the curtain went down on *Macbeth*. If Sir Carmichael was attacked at the theatre, during the play itself even, then that might arouse suspicion and draw attention to the whole plot. It was all a question of timing.

It was as he thought this that Arthur remembered the clock. If Art had somehow found himself in Arthur's body and time, then he would have Grandad to help him. To help himself, Arthur thought with a smile. He would remember the clock.

Normally he would have taken a bus to Jursall Street. But he didn't know if the numbers would be the same or where the bus stops were now. Or how much the ticket would cost, or even where he kept his money – if he had any.

There was surprisingly little traffic. The few cars there were seemed very noisy and travelled faster than the traffic he was used to in London – probably because there were no queues or jams. People seemed happy to walk in the road as much as on the pavement, and just about everyone wore a hat. A horse-drawn carriage clattered past and Arthur realised with a shock that this was a postman.

Jursall Street seemed not to have changed at all. Or rather, Arthur thought, it was the other way round – it would not change at all. The houses seemed a little less dilapidated, the paintwork less worn and peeled, the gardens less overgrown and neglected. But basically it was the same. He found the house he wanted and pulled back the wooden board so he could climb in through the front window.

He had been there several times before, of course – or rather he would come here in the future. Art had also been many times. They had both faced ghosts here, albeit of very different sorts. Arthur paused as he recalled previous visits, and he could hear the rumble of a tube train passing deep beneath the house as if to remind him. The noise increased as he opened the door under the stairs and started down the stone steps that led to the cellar.

This was where Art kept the clock. It was resting on a shelf at the back of an alcove. Arthur had not thought to bring a torch and he could barely see. There was some light from the open door at the top of the stairs. He waited for his eyes to adjust, then made his way carefully over to where he hoped the clock would be. He felt along the shelf, almost knocking the clock to the floor as his hand met its cold surface. But he managed to catch it and lifted it up close to his face. He considered taking the clock upstairs, but it was better to stay in the cellar, where they always met.

Art had kept the clock from a previous adventure – one involving a strange shop that sold clocks and watches. Very peculiar clocks and watches. In almost seventy years, Arthur would himself find the same clock – still on the ledge at the back of the alcove in the cellar. And when both boys wound the clock and its hands moved rapidly round the dial, then time seemed to fold up in this gloomy room so that the years between the two of them were as nothing and each appeared to the other.

They could talk, a bit. But always some things remained unsaid or unheard. Just as when he read the old casebook of the Invisible Detective Arthur was unable to recall certain details and

192

passages. Not until he was meant to – until whatever impact those events would have on his present had already taken place. Perhaps he had already read about his experiences back in the 1930s, or what the real Art was doing. He did not know.

The key turned more easily than usual and Arthur realised this was because the mechanism was newer. He set the clock down on the ledge, feeling carefully to be sure it was not at the edge, ready to fall off. Then he turned back towards the room and waited.

For a while nothing happened. He began to wonder if he had got it wrong. Did Art do something different to the clock? Did he have to wind it the other way, or move the hands or something? Or perhaps he just would not come to the cellar while he was in Arthur's time. If that was where – when – he was. Arthur had no way of knowing.

'Talking is only going to help so much.'

Arthur heard Art's voice before he saw him. Then it was a ghostly image – almost transparent.

'Grandad . . .' The pale image of Art laughed. 'Sarah says he's me, you know. It's strange, Let's hope it'll be over soon and we'll be back to normal. We'll swap back. At least, let's hope we will. If Grandad really is me, I suppose we must.'

'I suppose so,' Arthur replied. 'You're very faint, you know. I can hardly see you.'

'You too. I don't think we have very long.'

'It's all to do with the Castle Theatre, isn't it?' Arthur said. 'That must be the link. It's where *it* happened, after all.'

The faint image of Art nodded. He seemed even more ethereal now – as if he was made of morning mist and being dispersed by the growing light of the sun.

'We each have a mystery to solve,' Art said. 'I'll tell you what I know, what's happening, so you can carry on. You tell me what you're doing.'

Arthur nodded. 'I know you'll talk to Grandad, 'but have you told Sarah?' He wasn't sure why he wanted to know, but he was suddenly desperate to find out.

Art laughed. 'Didn't have much choice. She's quite headstrong, isn't she?'

'Yes, she is.'

'A bit like Meg.'

'Yes. I think we need to hurry.' He could

hardly see Art now. It was weird, seeing the boy dressed in modern clothes – in his own clothes, in fact. 'Should I tell the others?' he wondered. 'Meg and Jonny and Flinch?'

'Only if you have to,' Art said. 'I expect they'll soon have enough to worry about anyway. Now, then, this is what's been happening . . .'

He was tired when he got home and did not want to spend any more time with the real Art's father – his own great-grandfather – than he had to. So Arthur said he was tired, which was true, and went up to bed. At least having properly explored the house he now knew which was his room.

Strangely, he had found he was beginning to enjoy his situation. He could not imagine being trapped here in the past for ever – somehow he had to return, things had to be put right again. But he had the chance, however it might have happened, to meet the people he had read so much about. In a sense, he had already met Art by using the clock. Now he was spending time with Jonny and Meg and Flinch. He was one of the gang – a Cannonier.

As he settled down to try to sleep, Arthur

noticed that the drawer of the small wooden cabinet by the bed was slightly open. He reached out a hand to push it shut, then changed his mind. Instead, he opened it. And inside he saw a fountain pen and a book. It was a book he recognised instantly. A large notebook – the casebook of the Invisible Detective – exactly like Arthur's own copy but much, much newer. The cover was brighter and the pages less brittle. He leafed through it, reading the words he had read so often before, and marvelling at how much darker and clearer the ink and the pencil drawings and sketches seemed . . .

It reminded him of how he had been thinking about old photographs showing younger people. For a long, sad moment, he wondered what would happen to his new friends. He knew what happened to Art – to his grandad. But where were Meg and Flinch and Jonny back in his own time? He had asked Grandad, of course. But the old man's answers had been vague and evasive. Perhaps he really did not know. Perhaps they had lost touch. Or maybe Grandad did not want to say . . .

There were blank pages at the end of the

book, of course. Though it seemed that there was room for only perhaps one more case to be written up. Arthur stared for a while at the final entry in the notebook. It described the consulting session at which Mrs Foster had told of her daughter's experiences with the ghost at the Castle Theatre. Arthur picked up the pen and unscrewed the cap. He hesitated only a moment, then, in writing exactly like Art's, he wrote the date and under-lined it: *Saturday 24 April 1937.*

Beneath he wrote, 'It's me, Arthur. I don't know how, but here I am. The performance is tomorrow and we have to stop it somehow.' As he wrote, an idea occurred to him. An idea of how they could stop the audience being mesmerised. It was wild and dangerous, but it might just work. 'I have a plan,' he wrote in the casebook. But already his eyelids were so heavy they were shutting of their own accord.

He slumped back on to the pillow. His sleeping hand slid over the book, dragging the pen across the page, ripping deep into the paper.

'What we need is some sort of proof,' Arthur told them as they sat round on the rolls of dusty carpet

197

the next morning. 'We can't go to Sir Carmichael with a story about how people are going to be hypnotised at his theatre without any proof. He'd be very polite, but he'd think we were just plain daft.'

'But we can tell him what we know, what we've found out,' Flinch said. 'Charlie knows too.'

Arthur looked uncomfortable. 'That's another thing,' he said. 'Sir Carmichael would insist on checking things with Charlie.'

Meg said, 'I expect it's Charlie who has arranged all the VIPs who are coming.'

'And Charlie just keeps insisting that everything is fine and there's no problem.'

'But if we tell him . . .' Flinch began.

Jonny smiled at her insistence, and her confidence in Charlie. 'He's been got at. Can't we tell your dad?' he asked Arthur. 'The police could stop the play.'

Arthur shook his head. 'Again, we don't really have any proof. Even if we convinced him, he couldn't just call it off. He would still have to persuade Sir Carmichael and Charlie. He'd have exactly the same problem as we have.'

'So there's nothing we can do,' Meg said despondently. 'We can't persuade them to stop the performance, and we can't really interrupt it or stop it ourselves. Gregson would have us run out of the theatre or arrested, or worse.'

'Yes, I was thinking about that.'

'You've got a plan, haven't you?' Jonny said to Arthur.

Trust Art to have worked it all out. He really did seem almost back to normal. Jonny had begun to wonder if Art hadn't been hypnotised too, but today he seemed his old self – taking charge and organising their plan.

'Well,' Arthur said, 'it's just an idea. After all, it isn't the performance of the play that is the real problem. That isn't what we are trying to stop, is it?'

'No,' Meg said. 'If the conjuror weren't going to hypnotise everyone, they'd just enjoy the play.'

'Exactly. So that's the answer, isn't it?' Arthur was grinning as he told them his idea.

'You're joking,' Meg said when he had finished.

'I wasn't, actually.' Arthur shrugged. 'If you have a better idea – or any idea at all, come to that – then let's hear it.'

'Well, it's certainly a first,' Jonny conceded. He winked at Flinch. 'I don't think we've ever actually kidnapped anyone before.'

The note was handwritten in block capital letters. There was no time, date or return address. It had been folded in half and pushed under the door of his dressing room. John Prester – stage name Prester Digitation – read it again, wondering what it could mean.

IMPORTANT THAT WE MEET AT ONCE. I HAVE VITAL INFORMATION. COME TO THE OLD CARPET WAREHOUSE AT THE CORNER OF CANNON STREET AND ST SWITHIN'S LANE.

The note was signed, again in block letters: EDWARD WATLING.

There was no doubt in Prester's mind who the note was meant for. He felt cold as he read it a third time. *Edward Watling* – but Watling was supposed to be dead. A dead man requesting – demanding almost – a meeting. What could it mean? Prester folded the note and pushed it into his pocket. He had delayed too long already, he decided. It was time that something was done about Edward Watling. He took his coat from the hook on the back of the door and set off for Cannon Street.

It was late in the afternoon before Meg saw Jonny. She was leaning against the huge wooden doors at the front of the warehouse. They opened into St Swithin's Lane, though the bulk of the warehouse ran along Cannon Street. The wood of the doors had rotted at the bottom and bits had torn off, so that the base of the doors looked like a row of jagged teeth biting into the pavement. But the doors were locked and barred and there was no way that anyone could force their way through them.

Meg and the others did not have to, of course. They knew that there was a small door down the narrow alleyway that ran down the side of the warehouse. They knew just how to jiggle the door so that the lock on the inside jumped out of its socket and the door could be pushed open. But the conjuror – Prester – would not know that. So Meg was waiting for him at the front of the warehouse.

'He's coming,' Jonny gasped. He stood with

his head down, hands on his knees as he got his breath back. 'He caught a cab,' he explained. 'I had to run all the way. He can't be far behind.'

'You're faster than a cab?' Meg said in mock disbelief.

'Of course.'

Meg smiled. She knew that Jonny was fast. But he was not that fast. He had taken short cuts, nipped down alleyways that were too narrow for a car. He knew this part of London better than any taxi driver, who would only know the road system.

'You sure he's coming here?'

Jonny grinned. 'I heard him tell the cabbie where he wanted to go. He'll be here any minute. You wait.'

'I will. But you'd better not. Art and Flinch are ready inside. You'd better join them.'

'Right.' Jonny straightened up, took in a deep breath and ran off down the side of the warehouse.

He was right. Meg did not have long to wait. The cab dropped Prester on Cannon Street. She recognised him at once, although it wasn't hard. Being a Sunday afternoon the area was quiet and his was almost the only cab she had seen all afternoon.

Prester was taller than Meg remembered, though that might just be the effect of his top hat. He did not seem to recognise her, sparing her only a glance as he approached the warehouse. He tried the large iron handles on the doors. They rattled, but it was obvious they were not going to open. Prester sighed in frustration. He looked nervous, Meg thought – and well he might. He was coming, as far as he knew, to meet a man he had murdered.

He looked round again, and this time he paid more attention to Meg, standing only a couple of yards away. He touched his hat politely. 'Excuse me . . .' he started. Then he paused and frowned. 'Don't I know you?' He raised a finger, and Meg thought for a second he was going to put a spell on her. But he merely tapped it in the air for a moment as he recalled their previous meeting. 'Of course. You were at the theatre . . .' Again, his voice tailed off in realisation.

'Come with me,' Meg said, and turned towards the narrow alley. She paused to look back and check he was following. 'If you want to see Mr Watling, that is.'

Startled, Prester took a step backwards. Then

he seemed to gather himself, though he looked pale. 'How is he?' he asked in a husky voice.

'Come with me,' Meg said again, and led the way to the side door.

The door was standing open. Jonny must have forgotten to shut it. Or perhaps he had decided it would be better if the conjuror was not shown how to open the door, Meg thought. She said nothing, simply led the way inside.

'What is this place?' the conjuror asked as he followed Meg. She did not answer. He could see for himself what it was – an abandoned warehouse.

She was not taking him to the main storage area where the Cannoniers had their den. Instead she led him through to a corridor where there had been offices and storerooms. At the end of the corridor was a cage. It wasn't really a cage, but the end of the corridor could be closed off with an iron grille. Art had once suggested it might be where they locked up valuable items, like a large safe. The bars were rusty and brittle, but they were still strong enough. The heavy grille was folded back so that it was against the wall of the corridor – all but invisible unless you knew it was there.

Standing in the cage was a tall man. He had his back to them and Prester peered in to try to make him out. The light outside was fading as afternoon gave way to evening, and there was no artificial light in the warehouse. All that Prester would be able to see, Meg knew, was the vague outline of the man. A silhouette in the gathering gloom. Equally, he would not be able to make out the true nature of the shapes crouched beside the grille against the wall.

'Here he is, Mr Watling,' Meg said. She stood aside, well away from the grille so as not to alarm Prester, and gestured for him to come forward.

'Watling?' the conjuror said, his voice hesitant with nerves. He stepped forward. 'Edward Watling?'

There was no reply and he turned. Meg was afraid that he was going to walk away. She nodded back at the dark, silent figure, mentally urging Prester to go closer.

He took a step towards the figure. Then another. Still not quite enough. He stopped, started to turn again. 'What's going on here?' he demanded.

With a shriek, a shape leaped out of the

darkness and hurled itself at the man. Flinch's slight body collided with the conjuror. The surprise more than the impact knocked him back several paces. He crashed into the tall figure by the back wall, knocking the coat and hat from the long broom on which they were balanced. The broom handle clattered to the floor. Meg grabbed Flinch, pulling her clear just in time as Arthur and Jonny heaved the grille closed. It was heavy, stiff, screeching in protest as the hinges strained and rust flaked to the floor.

Prester gave a shout of anger and surprise and threw himself against the closing grille. He managed to stop it moving – just before the latch clicked into place. Arthur and Jonny were pushing with all their might, but slowly the iron door began to inch back open.

Then Flinch and Meg joined them, heaving with all their might. The door clicked shut and Flinch slipped a large padlock into place through a hole above the latch. She snapped it closed and they stepped away from the grille.

Prester stared at them through the bars, his pale face damp with sweat. The shadows of the grille made his whole form seem to flicker as he stepped forward and pushed furiously at the iron bars. They groaned and strained, but they did not move.

'What do you think you're doing?' Prester shouted. 'Let me out of here. Let me out at once!'

'No chance,' Arthur said, still breathing heavily.

'And let you hypnotise all those people?' Jonny told him. 'Not likely.'

'Like you hypnotised Edward Watling,' Meg put in.

'Watling?' He had given up pushing at the bars and put his shoulder to them. The whole grille seemed to bulge, but mercifully it held. 'Is that what this is about? Edward Watling?'

'You don't deny you knew him?' Arthur said.

'Of course I knew him. He came to the theatre to see . . .' Prester gave up, panting with the exertion. 'But he's dead. I read it in the paper.'

'So why answer his note? Why come here?' Meg demanded.

'I was intrigued,' Prester said. 'A note from a dead man – who wouldn't be?' He started pushing at the bars again, close to the hinges, but still with

207

no luck. 'And I came to warn him he was in danger.'

'In danger?' Flinch looked at Meg. 'What does he mean?'

'You have no idea what's going on,' Prester shouted at them. 'Let me out of here this instant.'

'With the performance due to start within the hour?' Arthur said. 'No way. You're staying in there until it's all over.'

'But why? What have you got against me?'

'You hypnotise our friends and you ask that?' Meg said angrily. She just hoped that after the performance Charlie – and anyone else under Prester's influence – would be returned to normal. 'Not to mention what you're planning for this evening at *Macbeth*.'

'Hypnotise?' Prester stared at her. 'Me?' He shook his head in apparent disbelief. 'I never hypnotised anyone in my life,' he said. 'And I'm not planning anything at the performance tonight. Apart from keeping well away from it.'

Meg stared at him. Beside her she was aware of Art, Jonny and Flinch turning to go. The plan had seemed simple – leave Prester locked up until after the performance. Then they would let him out and confess what they had done to Charlie and to Art's dad. It did not seem so simple now.

'Leave him, Meg,' Arthur was saying. He gently took her arm to lead her away.

'We can't,' Meg said. 'It's not that easy. We were wrong.' She felt cold and numb as she said it. But she knew – just as she always knew.

'What do you mean?' Arthur said. 'He's just bluffing. I mean – all that nonsense about not hypnotising anyone.'

'Except it's not nonsense,' Meg told him. 'We've made a terrible mistake, Art. You see, he's telling the truth. I *know* he is.'

'You know,' Arthur's grandad said, 'it's an odd thing, but I remember this meeting quite distinctly.' He smiled at Sarah and Art. 'I even remember when I was you, hearing me say that.' The smile stretched and his whole face seemed to be wrinkled up in amusement. 'And that too,' he added.

'I think we get the point,' Sarah told him. 'We could be here all day if you're not careful. And please don't tell us you knew I was going to say that.'

'I don't remember everything,' he confessed. 'It was a long time ago. But I do know this,' he said seriously to Art – to his younger self, 'there is very little I can or should tell you, apart from the fact that everything will be all right in the end. Time will make sure it works itself out, you wait and see.'

Art looked relieved, but Sarah could tell he was bursting to ask loads more questions.

'How long am I stuck here for?' he started.

Grandad stopped him with a raised finger. 'Wait and see,' he repeated. 'Just wait and see. Right now we have the Castle Theatre to worry about.'

He seemed to have assimilated Sarah and Art's hurried account of events there easily. Probably because, as Sarah now saw she should have realised, he had already experienced them himself, albeit nearly seventy years ago.

'You think we should stop the play? Tell them what happened?' she wondered.

'I doubt anyone would believe your story. And Art is right, there would be no evidence to back it up. No one else saw anything unusual, did they?' He already knew the answer, of course.

'But the performance of *Macbeth* that Sarah has told me about – it is significant?' Art asked.

'Oh, yes,' Grandad agreed. His smile had faded and his expression was serious once more. 'In just a couple of days, the play will go ahead and *Macbeth* will once again be performed in the Castle Theatre.'

'And we shall be there,' Sarah reminded them.

Grandad nodded grimly.

'You don't look as if you're looking forward to it much,' Art commented.

'No,' he admitted. He fixed his pale grey eyes first on Sarah, then on his younger self. 'No,' he said again solemnly. 'But then, I know what's going to happen.'

CHAPTER ELEVEN

Sir Carmichael's head was throbbing, but he did his best to ignore it. He didn't care what his doctor had advised, he was not going to miss the most important performance ever to be given in his own theatre. He had waved aside Charlie's arguments and eventually his old friend admitted that he had not expected Sir Carmichael to be able to stay away.

They took their seats in the royal box, although royalty would today be represented by His Majesty's Prime Minister, who was due to join them shortly. Then, in just a few minutes, the curtain would go up. He looked round at the audience already filling the auditorium. So many faces that he recognised – so many of the rich, important and famous. Here, in *his* theatre. It made him so proud. And what a setting, with the ornate columns and the caryatids holding up the gallery. The high vaulted ceiling made it look as much like a cathedral as a castle.

'Sir Carmichael.'

The voice brought him back to reality. He turned and rose, and shook the Prime Minister's hand. 'An honour, sir.'

'The pleasure is all mine.' The Prime Minister paused to shake Charlie's hand too. 'Fotherington – good to see you, as ever.' He took his seat, but the two men who had followed him discreetly into the box remained standing either side of the door. 'Yes, Sir Carmichael, I must say it promises to be a terrific event. And I've come prepared to enjoy myself.' He produced a slim volume from inside his jacket – a copy of *Macbeth*. 'Been doing my homework,' the Prime Minister told Sir Carmichael with a smile.

'Very commendable, sir. Certainly,' Sir Carmichael replied as he resumed his seat, 'I think it will be an evening to remember.'

'Look, it's not me that you want,' Prester insisted. 'Now will you kindly let me out of here?'

'I don't think we have any choice,' Arthur said. 'If he's telling the truth.'

'He is,' Meg confirmed. 'But not all of it,' she added. 'There's a lot he isn't saying.'

'Is that right?' Arthur asked.

Prester folded his arms and turned away from the grille.

'Please tell us,' Flinch said. She went up to

the grille, reached through and tugged at the man's sleeve. He turned back to face them, and Jonny gently pulled Flinch away, out of reach. 'Something terrible's going to happen if you don't.'

'Nothing terrible is going to happen,' Prester said abruptly. 'Now let me out or I'm going straight to the police.'

'Really?' Jonny said. 'To tell them what? That a few kids locked you up? Or that you're up to no good at the Castle Theatre?'

'I am not "up to no good", as you call it.'

'But you do know what's going on,' Arthur challenged.

Prester leaned on the bars and sighed. 'It's just to do with kudos. Just about making sure Herr Münster gets the acclaim he deserves for building Château Château. That his family gets the recognition.'

'Herr Münster?' Jonny said. 'I thought the château was in France.'

'Yes, but close to the border with Alsace. It was built by a German called Münster.'

'How do you know?' Flinch said.

'Yes,' Meg added. 'If you're not involved,

how do you know?' She took a step closer to the grille, watching Prester carefully. 'Are you Herr Münster's son?'

Prester blinked in what seemed like genuine surprise. 'His son? What are you talking about? I'm not German, I was born in Grimsby. Anyway,' he said, taking hold of the bars and shaking them violently, 'Münster's son is dead. He died in the flu epidemic in 1919. Now let me out!'

Arthur was holding the key to the padlock. But he hesitated, watching Prester suspiciously.

'He is telling the truth,' Meg said.

'Then how does he know so much about it?' Arthur wondered. 'About Münster and the castle and everything?'

'Oh, for goodness' sake!' Prester cried out. 'I know because Eva – Münster's daughter – worked with his son on stage until he died. That's why I got the booking at the Castle Theatre in the first place. She's my assistant in the act!'

'And that's all there is to it?' Arthur asked.

He had let Prester out of his prison and they were sitting on the rolls of carpet in the main area of the warehouse now. Prester had surprised them

215

by not immediately rushing off to find a policeman. He seemed tired and anxious and kept checking his watch.

'Yes, of course,' he said.

Meg cleared her throat. 'I know when you're lying,' she said.

Prester looked at her for a moment. Then he looked down at the floor. 'I don't know what she's doing,' he said quietly. 'I don't want to know.'

'She has to be stopped,' Arthur said. 'You have to help us.'

'Do I?' His face was drawn, with dark rings under his eyes when he looked up. 'She'll kill me if she finds out,' he said. 'Told me to stay away tonight and never go back. I was getting my things ready to leave when I got the note from Watling.'

'Watling is dead,' Arthur said.

'He jumped out of his window,' Flinch put in.

'Yes,' Prester said. 'Yes, I know. That's how . . . That's how I realised there was more to it than she had told me. I met Watling at the theatre. He came to see Eva after the show last week. He was behaving so oddly. Seemed so confused. She said that Watling was helping her,

216

but I could tell it wasn't willingly. I didn't realise till later – when I was watching Fred's hypnotism act. Then I knew what she was doing, what must be going on.'

'And you told no one?' Jonny said.

'Who would believe me?' Prester said sadly. 'Anyway, by then Watling was dead. I had no proof. Just a suspicion that she had taken him down to the cellar in the theatre and hypnotised him.'

'The cellar?' Arthur gasped in surprise.

'We store things for the act down there. The dressing room isn't big enough. I found her down there with Watling – he was just repeating the same phrase over and over. She would say it to him and he would chant it back.' He shivered. 'It frightened me. And she saw me and told me that . . .' He swallowed. 'That if I told a living soul, she would kill me.'

'And that was when she told you about wanting recognition for her family?' Meg asked.

Prester nodded sadly. 'Oh, what have I done?' he said in a small voice, and buried his head in his hands.

'I don't know,' Arthur said. 'I really don't.

But you have to tell us everything you know. Then we have to try to stop the performance.'

'You can't,' Prester said sadly. 'You're too late. It must be about to start.'

'Then tell us quickly,' Flinch told him.

'If I do, can I go?'

'We can't keep you here,' Arthur said. 'It's only your conscience that won't let you leave.'

Prester thought about his. He got to his feet and, for a moment, it looked as if he was going to leave. Then he took a deep rasping breath and turned back to face them all. 'I don't know what she is planning,' he said. 'But there are two things I can tell you.'

'Yes?' Meg prompted.

'She was not happy with Watling. Something went wrong. Something to do with controlling him. She said that unless she could solve the problem, then it would all have been for nothing. I wasn't really listening – I never really listened,' he admitted sadly. 'I didn't want to know. I thought if I ignored what she was doing it wouldn't affect me. But she said she could sense something. Some *lodestone*, I think she said. Something that would focus her mind. Then one day, last week, she showed me a stone. Like a pebble, only it sort of caught the light and shone it back in patterns. I didn't ask what it was . . .'

'We know about the pebble,' Jonny said. 'And where she got it.'

'She disguised herself and went to Jerrickson's shop,' Meg said.

'And the other thing?' Arthur asked.

'There was an old man who came to the theatre to see Mr Gregson yesterday. She saw him from the dressing-room door and said he was important.'

'Charlie!' Flinch said.

Prester shook his head. 'Lord something-or-other.'

'Lord Fotherington,' Meg told him.

Prester nodded. 'Yes. Anyway, she said that she wanted to talk to him, that he could help her. So I . . .' He turned away again, and when he spoke his voice was quiet and trembling. 'I took him to her. Down to the cellar. I didn't wait to see what happened. I didn't want to be involved. I still don't want to be involved.' His voice became a mutter, meaningless and garbled and punctuated by his sobs as Prester ran from the warehouse.

*

Jonny was already at the theatre by the time Arthur and the others arrived. He was waiting at the main door. The road was busy, Arthur saw – cars parked along the kerb, chauffeurs sitting smoking inside as they waited for the play to finish so they could drive their charges to their next destinations. Somewhere here was probably Charlie's car, with Weathers, his manservant, waiting patiently. But there was no time to look. If everything had been on schedule, then the performance had started nearly half an hour ago.

'What do we do?' Jonny asked as soon as they caught up with him. 'I've not seen anyone go in or come out. They must have started.'

'We have to see what's going on in there,' Arthur said. 'Come on.'

'Will they let us in?' Flinch wondered. 'We don't have tickets.'

That was a good point, and Arthur was prepared to dash past the commissionaire and the ticket lady and whoever else was waiting in the foyer.

But there was no one. The theatre foyer was empty.

'You'd expect someone to be here,' Meg whispered.

The double doors from the foyer into the main theatre were closed. But from the other side they heard the noise of collective laughter.

'Is it meant to be funny?' Jonny asked, with obvious relief.

Arthur felt the same. If the audience was laughing, then things couldn't have gone too wrong. 'There are some funny bits,' he told them. 'Well, teachers think they're funny. Stuff with a comedy porter.'

'Porters? Are there trains, then?' Flinch wanted to know.

But Meg waved her to silence and they all crowded round as Arthur eased open the main doors.

Arthur had a clear view down the main aisle to the stage. The performance was in mid-flow. Three witches stood round a cauldron and two men were close by – Macbeth and Banquo – meeting the Weird Sisters on the heath, Arthur thought as he tried to recall details of the play. But surely that came near the beginning. They should be further through than that.

Then he realised that the actors were not moving. They were not speaking their lines. They didn't even seem to be breathing, they were so still. Frozen into position, caught in an instant in time. The theatre was still and silent. The audience too was quiet – unnaturally quiet.

He turned to the others, his expression grave. He was about to speak, when the whole theatre erupted into sudden applause, making them all jump with surprise. Then, as abruptly as it had started, the clapping stopped. Still the actors on the stage did not move or speak.

'What's going on?' Meg asked in a harsh whisper.

'I don't know,' Jonny hissed back.

'Everything's stopped,' Flinch said, louder than the others.

'I think we're too late,' Arthur replied.

His voice sounded loud in the silence of the auditorium. No one turned to look.

Slowly, nervously, they walked up the main aisle towards the stage. Everywhere they looked, the people in the audience were sitting absolutely still and quiet. Then, just as it seemed they must be in some trance, they all reacted – together, at the same moment. A smile, a laugh, exchanged looks. As if they were caught up in the magic of a performance that Arthur and the others could not see.

'What's happened to them?' Flinch asked.

'They think they're watching the play,' Jonny said. 'They think it's still going on. Isn't that right, Art?'

But Arthur did not reply.

'Art?' Meg said.

They were almost at the stage now. Close enough to see that the witches and the two men were frozen in position. Close enough to see that there was a fourth woman close to the cauldron now – not standing hunched and silent like the other crones, but upright. Striding across the stage from the back to stare down at Arthur and his friends.

It was Eve – Prester's assistant. Eva, he had called her. She looked, Arthur thought, like a version of Lady Macbeth from a horror movie. Her eyes were shadowed with dark make-up, her lips were painted blood red, and her fingers with their long nails had curled into talons as she reached the front of the stage and let out a hiss of anger.

'How good of you to come,' she said, her eyes narrowing into blackness.

Slowly, as if waking from a deep sleep, the witches at the cauldron turned to look at Arthur and the others. At the same time the two men drew their swords and started towards the front of the stage, moving to the sides of the orchestra pit that created a barrier between the middle part of the auditorium and the stage.

Eva smiled. 'Such a pity that we can never let you leave here alive.'

The audience started to applaud, and the two swordsmen jumped down from the stage.

There was a temptation to go out and explore. But everything seemed so totally different that Art stayed at home for the most part. Sarah was good enough to come round and keep him company. Together they watched television – which was a novelty in itself. And it was in colour. It was rare enough for Art to see a colour film at the pictures. Everything they watched was noisy and fast.

When Sarah's telephone rang, he had no idea what was happening. It wasn't a bell like a real telephone – it played a tune. And the phone itself was so small. It fitted into the palm of her hand, and there were no wires. She could dial directly, without going through the operator.

'It takes digital pictures too,' she told him. 'And of course I text a lot.'

He didn't ask what she meant, it was all getting too complicated for words. She had showed him the computer in the spare room upstairs, but he had no idea what it was and the more she tried to explain the more unlikely and complex and incomprehensible it all sounded.

They talked a lot – about the Invisible Detective; about Jonny and Meg and Flinch.

'You miss them, don't you?' she said at one point. From the way she said it, he knew that she was thinking about the Arthur Drake that she had lost.

'You'll get him back,' he reassured her. 'We know that. You miss him too.'

She brushed her hair out of her eyes. 'Don't be daft.'

Arthur's dad was working that weekend, which was a relief. His own dad had been due at the office all weekend as well. It was odd how many similarities there were between the two Arthurs' lives, as well as how many differences. Both their fathers were policemen. They lived in the same house – just son and father. They both had friends they could rely on, he realised, looking at Sarah.

'Meg and Jonny and Flinch will look after him,' he said.

Sarah nodded, biting her lower lip. 'I know they will,' she said quietly.

Sarah found it both fascinating and frustrating being with Art. He was so like Arthur, yet so different. Of course he looked exactly the same – a different mind in the same body. But his outlook and background were worlds away. You wouldn't think so much could have changed in less than seventy years. But he glazed over when she tried to explain computers, and he looked ready to run and hide when her mobile rang.

Despite that, and her worry about what was happening to the real Arthur – her Arthur – she enjoyed being with him. Somehow it was easier and more relaxed being with someone she knew was not Arthur. That was weird too.

Sunday evening soon came round – and the performance at the Castle Theatre. She approached the event with trepidation. Would they really be on television? What was going to happen that Arthur's grandad wouldn't tell them? And what on earth should she wear?

Mum seemed happy enough for Sarah to go once she knew that Grandad would be there. It was funny how Sarah thought of Art and Grandad as two different people. Something else that had changed out of all recognition in seventy years. She shuddered at the thought of getting old and what it would do to her.

'You have a nice time,' Mum told her on the way out. 'I'm jealous of you meeting that Miles Kershaw.'

'He's no big deal,' Sarah told her.

Sarah's young brother, Paul, appeared behind their mother. 'She'll be with her boyfriend anyway,' he said.

Sarah opened her mouth to deliver a suitably sarcastic put-down, but she couldn't think of one. And anyway, she couldn't be bothered, she decided. If that was what he wanted to think, then fine. That was Paul's problem.

'Bye, Mum,' she said. 'I'll tell you all about it later.'

Art Drake sat alone in his small room in the home. He was waiting for his grandson – who for now at least was really his younger self – and Sarah to collect him for the play. He was not worried about what would happen. He already knew. He had already done it.

He had wondered at the time how he would feel now, meeting his younger self. He remembered how old he had thought he looked. He had thought he would never get so old. And now, how quickly he seemed to have got here. He got stiffly to his feet, feeling his knee crack with the effort, and shuffled over to the mirror. The craggy, lined face that stared back at him was barely recognisable as an older version of the boy he was waiting for. He shook his head, at once sad and happy.

He was happy for Art – for the years he had ahead of him. For the adventures and the excitement he knew were to come. But he knew too that there would be less happy times. The war, the loss of friends . . . He would marry and have a family. But the tears welled up in his eyes as the old man remembered both his wedding day and his wife's funeral ...

Yes, the young Art Drake had so much yet to experience, so much to look forward to. So much potential to fulfil. So long as time played out events in the same way as he remembered from 1937, and his younger self did indeed get back there. But what about now? What about the old man standing alone in front of a mirror in a tiny room in a run-down old people's home? What had *he* to look forward to, he wondered?

As he stood wondering, he heard the sound of Sarah's laughter from the corridor outside. He heard his own younger voice, indistinct, through the door. And he realised that no matter how old he got, there were still magic and excitement and friendship in his world.

They all got a taxi from Grandad's. He was wearing a dark blue suit that Sarah thought probably hadn't seen the light of day for several years. The jacket was visibly creased from where it had been hanging in his small wardrobe.

There were already a lot of people arriving at the theatre. They all seemed to be decked out in their best clothes. Sarah smoothed her dress anxiously. Arthur – or rather Art, she reminded herself – squeezed her hand. Was he giving reassurance or wanting it?

There was a camera team waiting in the foyer, with huge, bright lights arranged beside them. It was the same group of people they had seen outside before – cameraman, soundman and woman with clipboard. They were filming the people coming into the theatre and, as before, Miles Kershaw was with them.

When he saw Sarah, Art and Grandad, Kershaw hurried forward and drew them aside. 'You must be Mr Drake,' he said, pumping Grandad's hand up and down enthusiastically. 'I'm so very pleased you could make it tonight.'

'Wouldn't miss it for anything,' Grandad replied.

'Do you, er, that is . . .' Kershaw blustered. 'The invitation?'

Grandad produced the original invitation from his jacket pocket. Sarah could see the patch of discoloration on the back where it had been glued into the casebook.

'Oh, that's wonderful.' Kershaw declined to take

it, instead waving at the woman with the clipboard. 'You keep hold of that,' he told Grandad. 'Moira, let's get a close-up of this. And a few shots of Mr Drake and his guests. We'll drop them into the edit later,' he explained to Grandad. 'Obviously it isn't live, we're doing a highlights thing for tomorrow evening. Hope you can watch it.' He beamed at them. 'This should be a night to remember.'

They had been given seats next to the aisle. Grandad insisted that Art have the end seat, with Sarah next to him. 'You may have to get out in a hurry,' he said, his eyes catching the light and sparkling with what might have been amusement.

'Will it really be a night to remember, like he said?' Sarah asked. She didn't expect Grandad to answer.

'Who knows?' he told them, and again she got the impression that he was rather enjoying himself. 'When you're as old as I am, memory is a funny thing. Actually,' he said quietly, leaning to whisper to her, 'I think I shall probably sleep through it all.'

The lights dimmed and the noise seemed to fade too as people finished taking their seats and waited expectantly for the curtain to rise.

'You OK?' Sarah whispered to Art.

He nodded. 'You?'

'I hope so.'

She was feeling nervous. She could hear the tension in her own voice. Although the theatre seemed normal enough now, she could not help remembering what had happened the last time they were here. The carved wooden figures that stood by the doorways here in the main auditorium were identical to the ones that had come to life on the floor above. For the moment, they were silent and still. Just statues. Sarah reached across and took Art's hand. He glanced at her and smiled. She could see he was nervous too, and that actually made her feel a bit better.

The curtain rose. The audience was silent. Three grotesque figures stood round a large cauldron in front of a backdrop of dark storm clouds. At the side of the stage a great pile of brushwood reached up almost out of sight. It seemed to represent the edge of a wood. Birnam Wood, Sarah thought – the wood that later seemed to move when the soldiers held branches in front of themselves for camouflage as they marched forwards. Balancing the wood on the other side of the stage was a stone wall – Macbeth's castle at Dunsinane.

'*When shall we three meet again?*' one of the witches demanded, her voice brittle and cracked like dry leaves.

There was a rumble of thunder. A flash of artificial lightning, like a camera going off. Sarah waited for the next line. But it never came.

The figures of the witches were frozen in position. Unmoving. Sarah looked at Art. He was frowning, waiting as she was for the next line of the play. Realising it was not going to come.

On the other side of Sarah, Grandad did not move. She nudged him with her elbow. 'What's going on?' she hissed. 'Why is no one reacting?' she asked, realising that the audience was as still and silent as the tableau on stage.

Grandad did not answer. He was staring glassily ahead. As was the woman on the other side of him. And the man next to her. Sarah looked round, aware that Art was doing the same. And everywhere they looked the audience was immobile, watching a play that was not happening. Unseeing, unmoving . . . Frozen in a trance.

'It's started,' Art said out loud. No one reacted.

The voice seemed to come from everywhere and nowhere, echoing round inside Sarah's head.

'*Now I rise again!*'

A woman's voice – both triumphant and relieved, speaking with a distinct accent.

'*The future in an instant.*'

And from Art's lack of reaction, Sarah was sure that only she had heard it.

CHAPTER TWELVE

'Run!' Arthur shouted.

Jonny did not need telling again. The woman – Eva – was holding up the stone she had taken from the locksmith's. She had it clasped between her fingers as if she was examining a rare jewel. She muttered something that Jonny did not catch. But in response, the two actors with swords advanced menacingly on Jonny and the others.

A sword flashed through the air, slicing past Jonny's face as he ran by one of the men. He felt the breeze from the sword and for a moment was afraid he had been hit. His hand went to his cheek, but it came away dry – no blood. Once past the man, he turned to see what the others were doing. His first instinct had been to run, but now he was worried for his friends. Should he go back and help?

Arthur had grabbed one of the men by the sword arm – intercepting the blade as it slashed towards him. He pushed the man away, allowing himself and Meg to duck under his flailing arm and run off to the opposite side of the stage from where Jonny was now standing.

But Flinch was trapped. She was between the two men. One was recovering from Arthur's attack, the other was stalking towards her, ignoring Jonny now that he was past him. Jonny did not hesitate. He ran at the man, launched himself at the actor's back. Seeing him rushing forwards, Flinch dropped into a crouch. The man stumbled under the impact as Jonny hit him. He tripped over Flinch, and cannoned into his colleague. They both collapsed in a tangle of arms – two swords stabbing in the air.

The woman was shouting – screaming at them in rage. Meg and Arthur were already out of sight, disappearing off to the side of the stage. The three witches round the cauldron – haggard old women dressed in stained, grey rags – turned towards where Jonny and Flinch were standing.

'Come on,' Jonny said, pushing Flinch ahead of him as he ran.

They dashed along the front row of the audience, climbing over immobile legs. Jonny glanced down into the orchestra pit as they rushed by. The half-dozen musicians were frozen like the audience – a violin bow was poised over the strings; a flute player's cheeks were puffed out slightly as he blew; the conductor's baton pointed accusingly at Jonny and Flinch as they pushed past.

Flinch's scream told Jonny something was wrong before he realised what was happening. The front row of the audience was moving. The people that Jonny and Flinch were pushing past were getting to their feet, reaching out . . . Jonny could see her shaking off the hands of an elderly woman. The woman's eyes were as sightless and milky pale as the pearls that hung round her neck.

Hands clutched and fumbled at Jonny too. He put his head down, closed his eyes and pushed. He shoved his way along, feeling fingers gripping his jacket and grabbing at his arms. He managed to shake them off, prised a man's hands away from his shoulder, wrestled and shouted and pushed and fought his way along the row of mindlessly clutching figures.

And suddenly he was past them. They turned to watch him go, but made no effort to follow. An urgent thump of footsteps alerted Jonny to another danger – one of the swordsmen was running across the stage. The man launched himself into the air – hurling himself forwards. Towards Jonny.

Sword stretched out. Jonny could see the lights high above glinting on the blade as it lanced towards him.

Jonny turned and ran. There was no sign of Flinch, so he just ran – up the aisle at the side of the auditorium. Through an exit door flanked by carved women and into a side corridor. Up the corridor. In his ears he could hear the rushing of his own blood, and the shouts of the magician's assistant as she gave orders from the stage, the thump of chasing feet and the cackle of the witches as they too joined in the hunt.

Flinch did not need to think about what to do. Instead of trying to get through the crowd, she dropped suddenly and quickly to the floor. The audience did not seem to realise she had gone and still reached out into the space above her. Clutching hands fought each other as they struggled to find her again, and Flinch wondered if the people could actually see at all.

Rolling quickly under the feet, Flinch recognised Jonny's shoes as they stamped past. They were making slow but certain progress and she knew he would be all right. At least for now.

The seats were sprung so that when people stood up their seats folded up too, to give more space between the rows. This gave Flinch room behind the row of standing people – just enough to squeeze herself under one of the chairs. It was tight getting between the iron supports that held the row of seats fixed to the floor, but she managed, just. Pulling herself through, she was faced with a row of legs – the next row of the audience, still sitting stock still and watching a play that was not happening.

Flinch forced aside the legs of a young man in military dress uniform and tumbled into the gap under his seat. She lay there, knees pulled up to her chin, listening to the shrieks of the witches, the angry cries of the magician's assistant and the ghostly breathing of the audience. Before long, the people in the front row sat down again. Flinch held her breath – would they look for her? Would the woman controlling them realise where she had gone? If anyone saw her, there was no way she could escape now. She was trapped behind a wall of legs, their dark shapes like the bars of a prison cell.

*

The ancient hags that chased after Meg and Arthur were cackling for all the world like real witches. Meg knew they were just actresses made up to look old and ugly. But she also knew that whatever the magician's assistant had done to them had the effect of making them believe that they really were witches. Who or what they thought Arthur and Meg might be, she did not wish to speculate.

Meg turned and ran – straight into a large figure standing in the wings. It was one of the stagehands; she recognised him from the group that had held them outside Gregson's office. Meg backed away. But Arthur grabbed her hand and pulled her onwards.

'It's all right,' he said. 'They're all frozen back here too.'

Meg could see now that the figures standing in the wings – stagehands, scene shifters, even a little old lady sat on a chair with a copy of the script ready to prompt actors who forgot their lines – were as immobile as the figures on stage and in the audience had been.

But not for long, she thought. Not if Eva Münster realised where they had gone. Meg had seen the front row of the audience grabbing mindlessly at Jonny and Flinch. It would take only a thought focused through the strange pebble to send the backstage staff stalking after Meg and Arthur.

Arthur seemed to have realised this too, and with renewed urgency they both ran round to the back of the stage. There was a gap between the heavy canvas that hung down there and the wall of the corridor behind. The stage ended at the canvas, so they were below the level of it now, in a trench that ran along the back.

'Maybe we can hide, until we work out what to do,' Arthur said. 'But if we stay here we'll be trapped.'

'How's she managed to hypnotise them all?' Meg asked him. 'Even the people back here.'

'Everyone within earshot, I should think.' Arthur was frowning, looking for somewhere to hide.

'Maybe we can get under the stage?' Meg suggested.

She ran her hand along the wooden back of the stage, but there did not seem to be any way to get through – no trap doors or openings.

'It must be to do with the play,' Arthur was saying. 'She's somehow put everyone into a state where she can use the repeated lines of *Macbeth* to control them, focused using that stone.'

'So how do we stop her?'

Arthur opened his mouth to answer. But what came out instead was a cry of warning. It was almost drowned by the sound of tearing fabric. The canvas was being ripped apart above them, threads and flaps falling into the trench behind the stage. The tearing sound became the cackle of the witches as they ripped their way through the backdrop. Dark eyes searched out Meg and Arthur, fixed on them. Then three screaming, ghoulish figures leaped down off the raised stage.

Arthur pushed Meg along the narrow trench, out of the way of the first witch, who landed with a shriek of delight between them.

'Run for it!' Arthur screamed.

Meg ran. She felt a hand snap at her, felt talon-like nails catch in her hair as it streamed out behind her. Felt herself falling backwards and snapped her head forward to try to break loose. Suddenly she was free, but she could still feel something pulling in her hair – tangled and caught. As she ran she scrabbled to get rid of it, caught it in her hand, glanced at what she had dislodged. And screamed.

It was a long, bloodstained fingernail. She dropped it and ran on.

'It's not real,' she gasped to herself as she ran. 'Just make-up. Glued on. Paint, not blood.'

She risked a look back – to see if Art was following her. She caught a glimpse of him as he escaped round the other end of the stage, two of the witches hurrying after him with their ragged clothes blown back. The other witch was close to Meg, grinning manically as she chased after her. Meg turned back and ran on.

The end of the trench was blackness – a wall. She was trapped.

With a sob of fear and frustration, Meg skidded to a halt, pounded her fists into the black wall.

And found that it billowed away under the impact – a curtain.

Behind her the witch cackled and laughed and reached hungrily for Meg's hair.

'Not again,' Meg said. 'Not this time, Grandma!' She grabbed the black curtain and pulled with all her might, wrenching it off the hooks high above.

The falling curtain was a wave of blackness. With one hand over her head to ward it off, the other pushing away the witch's attempts to grab her, Meg leaped forward. The curtain fell behind her, crashing down on the witch, smothering her shrieks of anger. A dark mass writhed and thrashed as the witch struggled to escape. Meg paused only long enough to kick the shape to the floor and wrap the curtain more firmly over the top. Then, she was running again.

When it was quiet, Flinch dared to pull herself out from under the seat. The soldier did not seem to mind that she dragged his feet apart to make room for her to crawl from under his seat. He did not object when she knelt up and peered carefully between the two people sitting in the row in front.

The stage was deserted apart from the magician's assistant, who was standing at the front of the stage, close to the pit where the musicians played. She held Mr Jerrickson's stone up in front of her face and seemed to be staring at it. Or into it. The stone was the key, Flinch thought. If the woman put it down, maybe Flinch could somehow get hold of it. But how? She needed to be closer, not stuck here in the middle of an audience that could at any moment be turned against her. She remembered the hands that had clutched and tugged at her, and she shuddered.

The woman looked up from her study of the stone and stared out into the audience, a smile of triumph on her painted face. Her voice was loud and clear, with the trace of an accent which Flinch assumed must be German.

'Very well,' she said. 'Despite the interruption, I think we are ready to proceed. Many of you have important tasks, which I shall now give you. Then you will leave here and go about your business as if nothing has happened. Nothing but a play.' She gave a short staccato laugh. 'You will think that you have but slumbered here, while these visions did appear. That you were watching the play, and if you missed anything it is because you perhaps slept for a moment or two. Nothing more. Any memories you might retain . . . Well . . .' She shrugged. 'The earth hath bubbles as the water has, and these are of them.'

As she spoke, she carefully got down from

the stage. She was standing now at the front of the audience. She took another step forwards, looking along the front row. Her eyes had narrowed as she looked at each member of the audience in turn. Looking perhaps, Flinch thought, for particular people. But when she came to the next row, she would see Flinch.

As quickly and quietly as she could, Flinch ducked back under the soldier's chair. She pushed herself out the other side and into the next row. But she could not keep doing this. It would take too long, and eventually she would reach the back of the theatre.

A quick glance told Flinch when the woman turned to look along the other side of the theatre. As soon as she was looking the other way, Flinch jumped to her feet and ran. But the woman was already turning back. There was no way that Flinch could reach any of the side doors in time to avoid being seen. Jonny could have done it. But she was nowhere near as fast as Jonny.

So instead she ran for the stage.

The woman continued to turn, frowning as she caught sight of a blur of movement from the corner of her eye. Suddenly she snapped round – staring at the stage behind her.

But there was no one there. And no one could have got across the stage and out to the wings or through the torn backdrop without her seeing. Eva Münster spent a moment pondering the possibilities.

It must have been her imagination, she decided. She had enough to concentrate on, keeping the audience entranced and controlling the minds of the people hunting for the children. She smiled as, in her mind's eye, she saw that one of them at least had been found.

Charging along the corridor, Arthur could hear the witches close behind him. He could hear their dry cackles of laughter, the slap of their bare feet on the stone floor, the rasping of their breath. He imagined he could feel their hot breath on the back of his neck, but he dared not turn to see how close they really were.

With relief he realised that the sounds were growing quieter, not louder. He was drawing away from them. If he could get far enough ahead he could find somewhere to hide and catch his breath and think what to do next. The storeroom where Flinch had pretended to be a ghost was just ahead. The corridor turned slightly before it, and if he was quick he might be able to get inside and close the door before the witches realised where he had gone. They would go running past.

Spurred on by this plan, Arthur increased his speed, the flagstones on the floor passing in a blur.

There was the door – just ahead. And it was open, which would save him time. Arthur slowed, ready to dart inside.

But the door was open because there was already someone in the storeroom. Waiting. Stepping out into the corridor in front of Arthur. Raising a sword, so that Arthur had to lurch to a painful halt to avoid being skewered on the end of it.

Macbeth. His eyes dark and ringed with make-up. His expression blank, but his sword unwavering. Arthur could hear the laughter of the Weird Sisters as they approached behind him.

Macbeth's dark eyes glinted like the blade of his sword as he levelled it at Arthur. The man's voice was a harsh whisper, grating on Arthur's frayed nerves:

'Will all great Neptune's ocean wash this blood clean from my hand?'

The point of the sword bit into Arthur's chest.

The play had started up again. It was like a film grinding slowly into life as the projector runs up to speed, Art thought. The three witches jerked back into motion.

'Thrice the brinded cat hath mew'd,' one of the hags intoned.

Sarah was shaking her head, as if she was getting a headache. As the witch spoke, she looked up. 'That's not right.'

'What do you mean?' Art asked her. Nothing here was right.

'Thrice and once the hedge-pig whined,' another witch said.

'That comes later on in the play. We've jumped forward. She's changed it.'

'The witch?'

'The woman in my head,' Sarah said. Art had no idea what she meant, but her eyes were wide and anxious. 'I don't know what's going on, but we have to stop it.' She was shouting now, above the cackle of the witches as they danced round the cauldron. But no one reacted except Art.

'Come on, then!'

He pulled her out of her seat and they ran towards the stage, shouting at the actresses to stop. But they got no reaction. The women were no longer acting – they had *become* the witches.

All three of them turned and stared malevolently at Art as he clambered up on to the stage, close to the enormous pile of wood. '*Double, double toil and trouble,*' they chanted. '*Fire burn, and cauldron bubble.*'

But the words were almost drowned out by the wrenching and splintering of wood. All round the auditorium the caryatids by the doors were tearing themselves free. The theatre echoed to the sounds of the wood snapping and breaking, the creaking of their movements like trees in the wind. A lamp slammed suddenly down from high above and shattered close to where Art was now standing on the edge of the stage. Sparks showered across the stage as the bulb exploded.

Then the curtain came crashing down. Art grabbed Sarah and pulled her further on to the stage and out of the way as the heavy material fell. In front of them, the witches circled and chanted menacingly. Beside them the pile of brushwood reached up so high the top was lost in the glare of the lamps hanging from the metal lighting gantry. Behind them the audience looked on and saw nothing.

The wooden figures were lurching uncertainly towards the stage. But with every step they seemed to become more confident – more accustomed to movement. Whatever Art and Sarah were going to do, they had to do it now.

'She's coming back,' Sarah said. Her voice was almost a sob and her hands were clenched to her head. 'She's here. She's always been here. And now . . .' Her words dissolved into a scream of pain and anguish as she collapsed to her knees. 'Help me!' she gasped.

'*For a charm of powerful trouble, like a hell-broth boil and bubble.*'

Art backed away from the witches, reaching down to try to help Sarah. A whole section of the stage suddenly fell away, and he staggered to avoid falling into the gaping hole – a trap door, he realised. He felt Sarah's hand, felt her clutch at him, pulling herself back to her feet.

He dared to look away from the witches and the trap door, and was relieved to see that Sarah's face had cleared. Her hands were no longer at her head and she seemed to be back to her normal self.

'Thank goodness,' he gasped.

Despite the situation, she smiled at him. It was a strange half-smile, and Art could see it echoed in the faces of the approaching caryatid figures as the first of them reached the edge of the stage. Sarah was still holding his arm, he realised.

'Goodness has nothing to do with it,' she said quietly.

The witches cackled with glee. One of the statues hauled itself awkwardly up on to the stage and stood swaying slightly as it regarded Art with blank eyes.

Sarah's eyes were the same – dark and blank, he realised. Like polished wood. She let out a screech of laughter and shoved him suddenly and violently towards the hole in the stage.

CHAPTER THIRTEEN

'You know what this is, don't you?' Eva Münster held up the pebble so that it caught the light, reflecting a myriad of colours and almost dazzling Arthur with its brilliance. 'I can tell,' she assured him. 'I know. I can feel it.'

'Is that how you found it?' Arthur demanded.

The sword was scratching his back as Macbeth urged him onward, across the stage. The three witches circled him as he moved, their fingers writhing like snakes.

'Of course. I could sense its power. I needed its power.'

'Because you aren't strong enough on your own,' Arthur said.

He was hoping to keep her talking. If she was telling him what was going on, that might give him time to find a way to escape.

Eva waved the witches away. 'Go and find the others,' she ordered.

Still laughing, the hags spun and shambled across the stage, disappearing into the wings. There was just Eva now, and Macbeth, and the sword.

Arthur swallowed, looking round desperately for help. But there was no sign of any of his friends. The audience watched impassively. He could·see Charlie sitting beside Sir Carmichael in a box at the side of the stage, slightly raised above the main auditorium. There was another man sitting with them, and two men in suits stood either side of the back door to the box. None of them seemed to see Arthur or have any idea of what was really happening. He could imagine a version of *Macbeth* playing out in front of them, like a film slid in between the audience and reality.

'What do you know about this stone, Art Drake?' she asked

Arthur gaped. 'How do you know my name?'

'You told me. Don't you remember?'

He didn't. But then, she had probably spoken to the real Art, not to him. After the variety show perhaps, when the children had gone backstage. 'I know the stone focuses the power of the mind,' he told her defiantly. 'I know that Bessemer's puppets were controlled using it. And I know that you couldn't hypnotise Edward Watling properly without it.'

Her dark eyes narrowed. 'Watling,' she murmured. 'Such a willing subject. A good subject too – so much he could tell the Reich. And yet you are right. Away from my influence, his mind learned to wander. My power faded.'

'He went through his programmed task without being triggered by you.'

She frowned. 'Programmed?'

'I mean, he did what you had ordered him to. But not when you wanted it. Anyone could set him off in the right circumstances.' Arthur stepped forward, and felt the prick of the sword ease from his back. Maybe there was still a chance. Maybe he could run for it.

'Yes,' Eva was saying. 'I needed the stone to focus the power.'

'You really think your plan will work?'

'I know it will work.' Her face creased into a smile. Blood red lips parted in anticipation of her own words. 'You see, I tested it. I would not set this up without being sure.' She waved her hand across to indicate the still and silent audience. 'I had a very good test subject.' Her teeth seemed stained red by the lipstick, so it looked as if her mouth was full of blood. 'Oh, he fought, he struggled, but he could not resist. Even though he was aware of the power of the stone and knew what I was doing.'

Arthur felt suddenly cold. 'You mean Charlie,' he said.

She shook her head, her smile wider and more grotesque than ever. 'No. He was easy, a simple autonomic response implanted in the front of his mind. No, I did not test the full extent of my ability to control the mind on him.' She took a step forwards, pointing straight at Arthur's face. 'I tested it on you.'

Flinch peeped carefully out from her hiding place. She had a clear view of Art, and of the man with the sword standing behind him. Across the stage, the magician's assistant looked triumphant. She didn't have a sword or a gun or anything so far as Flinch could see. If she could distract the man with the sword, then maybe Art could escape.

'Of course, you don't remember,' the woman was saying. 'You surprised me, in the cellar. I was practising the words and phrases I would use to prime my subjects. Rehearsing, if you like.' She laughed at the comment. 'And now we meet for the *final* performance.'

'Of course I don't remember,' Arthur said quietly, as if to himself.

'Because I instructed you not to. Just as now,' she lifted her hand, 'I tell you to remember.' She snapped her fingers, like a gunshot. As the echoes of the sound died away, she said, '*Come, thick night, and pall thee in the dunnest smoke of hell.*' She spread her arms in triumph. 'You remember now.'

Flinch could not see Art's expression. But she could imagine the horror on his face as he recalled whatever had happened in the cellar.

'You remember everything now,' the woman went on with evident glee. 'You remember seeing me amidst the candles. How you tried to run, but I caught you. You remember my words eating into your mind and the blackness that swept in and darkened everything. Everything except what I said to you. Everything except your instruction – to forget until you heard a certain phrase. To obey me without question when you heard another.'

Arthur's voice was hoarse and ragged. 'Do

you use the same phrase to trigger all your victims?'

'Of course,' she admitted. 'To prime them, and then to have them obey my will. For the good of the Fatherland. For the Reich. But for the people here tonight the key is more than the simple phrase I used on you. I cannot afford the chance that, like Watling, they will hear a few words and react without my knowing it.' She turned a full circle, arms outstretched. 'Everyone here is as you were in the cellar. In a waking dream. Neither seeing nor hearing reality. In a world of their own.'

'What,' Arthur said slowly, 'if you never give them instructions? If you trigger them without ever telling them what to do? Will they recover?'

The woman threw back her head and laughed. 'You are so transparent,' she said. 'You still think you can stop me? You cannot even escape.'

As she laughed, she took a step backwards, away from Arthur. Was it far enough? Flinch was not sure. But she was sure that if she did not help Art soon, she would lose the chance. The swordsman was still standing a short distance behind Art. Flinch hoped it was far enough. She took a deep breath and leaped out of the cauldron.

All Arthur saw was a flash of movement out of the corner of his eye. It was like a trick of the magician's – one moment nothing, the next Flinch hurtling towards Macbeth and shouting at Arthur to run.

Eva's expression had darkened from triumph to rage and she screamed something incoherent in German.

Macbeth did not react. Not until Flinch hit him like a steam train. Then he flew backwards. He made no attempt to break his own fall, landing heavily on his back without so much as a groan. The sword clattered to the floor beside him. Flinch rolled head over heels, coming to a stop almost at the edge of the stage.

Arthur was already running – racing across the stage after Flinch. 'Run!' he shouted. 'Find Meg and Jonny.'

Flinch uncurled, and seemed to slide off the stage and out of sight into the orchestra pit. There must be a way out of the pit, Arthur realised. A door for the musicians and the conductor. He was almost close enough to leap down after Flinch. Almost.

But Eva Münster was shouting after him. Her voice grated in his ears, seemed to slow and slur as the words seemed to spread through his whole being.

'By the pricking of my thumbs . . .'

He shook his head to get rid of the feeling. It's just in my mind, he told himself. She can't control me. It's my imagination. She thinks she can, but she can't. *She can't.*

In front of him, Macbeth was clambering to his feet, scooping up the sword, turning to face Arthur. The sword swung up and Arthur skidded to a halt.

'. . . Something wicked this way comes.'

And remained absolutely still, the sword an inch from his throat.

Eva walked slowly across to where Arthur and Macbeth were standing. 'You cannot resist me,' she told Arthur.

He did not reply. He did not move. He did not even look at her.

'And now, I see, you are ready for your instructions.' She tapped a long, painted fingernail against her lips. Blood red on blood red. 'I really cannot afford to have you attempting to escape or trying to interfere.'

She turned to survey the stage, looking all round. Then she looked up, towards the high gantry where the lights were hung. It was like a narrow walkway running across the top of the theatre, thirty feet above the stage.

'Yes,' she decided, turning back to the immobile Arthur. 'Perhaps you will benefit from a little demonstration of the power I have. The power over you. And soon, over all of the people here – the people of power and influence who can help Germany in the glorious times ahead.' She nodded to herself, pleased with the thought. 'I want you to climb up to that gantry. There is a ladder at the side of the stage.' She nodded to Macbeth. 'Go with him, as far as the ladder. Watch him climb.'

Slowly, stiffly but inexorably, Arthur turned and walked across to the wings. He took hold of the rough wooden sides of the ladder without a word. He started to climb.

Below, on the stage, the magician's assistant watched and smiled. 'When you get to the gantry,

261

go to the middle of it,' she called up to him. 'Then I want you to jump. Jump as far out as you can. See if you can reach the orchestra pit. But if you don't make it that far, if you don't kill yourself, don't worry.' She laughed again, an echoing, evil burst of sound. 'At the very least you will still break both your legs.'

Arthur stood at the top of the ladder, ready to step on to the gantry. He looked out over the theatre. Far below, the audience seemed to be waiting expectantly.

The hole in the stage was a black mouth about to swallow him up as Sarah pushed him. But somehow Art managed to turn his stagger into a leap across it. His foot caught on the far edge of the trap, slipped, fell into the hole. He braced his other leg, sprawled sideways, scrabbled desperately with his hands, aware of the witches closing in. He managed to haul himself up and out of the hole, falling across the stage.

'You think you can escape so easily?' Sarah

laughed at him. Her voice was strange – older, deeper, accented . . .

There were several of the statues on the stage now, lumbering towards him. Their wooden dresses moved only where attached to the legs, making them look even more awkward and strange.

'I have waited so long for this,' Sarah was saying. 'Waited and slept. But now the words have awakened me. The rehearsals began the process and now, finally, the words – the trigger phrase – will give me life. Just as I planned. Just as I knew they would. I shall no longer be imprisoned within the fabric of this building – my mind trapped inside my father's creation.'

The witches circled round Art, leaning towards him, spitting their words into his face. The caryatids formed an outer circle, closing slowly in. If they kept coming, they would eventually crush him.

'*Scale of dragon, tooth of wolf . . .*'

He couldn't stop them, Art realised. Not alone. But maybe he could escape, maybe he could wake Grandad – himself. He had to survive this somehow. Had to, in order to be sitting entranced out there in the audience. The realisation gave him energy and confidence. Almost without thinking, he threw himself between two of the chanting witches – right at one of the statues.

It was like running into a wall. The breath was knocked out of him, and he staggered and gasped. But the statue was thrust backwards by the impact. Just as Art had hoped. It teetered for a moment on the edge of the hole in the stage, made no attempt to save itself, fell – like a piece of wood.

Before it had disappeared from sight, Art had recovered and was leaping after it – over the hole rather than into it. He hoped that his speed would carry him past Sarah, or what she had become, before she realised what was happening.

But just as he thought he was free and had escaped, right at the edge of the stage, next to the huge pile of brushwood, his legs stopped working. He felt the energy drain from him. For a moment, he stood still, wondering what was happening. His brain was willing, urging him to move, but nothing happened. It was as if his body was not his own.

Then he did start to move, to walk. Slowly, but without any conscious decision, he walked into the wings. The wooden figures turned to follow. Sarah was screeching at them to get him. His mind was desperately, but ineffectively, ordering his body to

stop. Unable to control himself, Art began to climb the ladder up to the lighting gantry, high above the stage.

CHAPTER FOURTEEN

Jonny arrived in the auditorium in time to see Eva Münster order Art to climb up to the gantry and jump. At the back of the theatre, he held his breath as he watched. He looked round desperately for something – anything – that could break Art's fall. He knew he was fast, but even he could not get to the stage before Art reached the middle of the precarious walkway and leaped to his death.

Art was on the gantry now, walking carefully along the narrow metal mesh. There was a low railing either side, but when he turned to jump it would not stop him. Jonny watched, frozen in horror. He became aware that Meg was standing close to him, also watching. She had been hiding behind the back row of the audience.

'We have to do something,' she hissed.

But Jonny just shook his head. Maybe Flinch could help, but he had seen her tumble into the orchestra pit, out of sight. Did she even know what was happening?

Art stopped in the middle of the gantry. Jonny held his breath.

But Art did not jump. Instead, he shouted out

in a clear, calm voice, '*By the pricking of my thumbs, something wicked this way comes.*'

The audience seemed to react to the words. Jonny could see people stiffen, as if sitting suddenly to attention. But the spell was not broken, they did not wake.

'You need to say more than that!' Meg shouted. She was running towards the stage. 'She said – you need the whole speech.'

What speech, Jonny wondered? Presumably the words that led up to that point. But what were they? And how much of the play did Art need to recite to wake the people?

Jonny ran after Meg, catching her up easily, craning his neck to see what Art was doing, high above them.

'*Double, double toil and trouble,*' Art shouted out. '*Fire burn, and cauldron bubble.*'

'That's it,' Meg gasped, struggling to keep pace with Jonny.

Around them, the people in the audience were shifting and stirring, like they were bored with the performance and ready to go home.

But Art had stopped. He didn't know any more, Jonny realised with a sinking feeling. He staggered to a stop, putting his arm out to stop Meg as well. It would do no good for them to get caught.

But the woman was ignoring them. Obviously considering Art the main threat to her plans, she was staring malevolently up at him. 'You'll have to do better than that,' she snarled.

With a vehement wave of her arm, she directed the actor with the sword to start up the ladder after Art. Then she turned and marched to the other side of the stage. Jonny saw her pause and snatch something from the old woman sitting in the wings, before she reached for the ladder on that side of the stage and started to climb. Opposite her, Macbeth mirrored her actions – hand over hand, his sword dangling by his side.

'He's trapped. We have to help him,' Meg said urgently.

The audience had settled back into silence once more.

Jonny wondered what they could possibly do. Then he saw it. 'Quick!' he shouted to Meg, and leaped up on to the stage.

The huge backdrop that showed a thunderous sky had been ripped apart in the middle, where the witches had torn through it as they chased after Meg and Art. Jonny grabbed the torn edge of the heavy canvas.

'Get the other end,' he called to Meg.

'Why?'

'Just do it! We have to drag it to the front of the stage.'

She ran to grab the end of the backdrop, right at the edge of the stage. It swung forward easily, secured only at the top. Together Meg and Jonny ran back across the stage, dragging the canvas with them, or rather half of it. The material ripped up the middle, from the existing tear, as Jonny heaved it across the stage. It got harder the further they ran, as they pulled more weight. And the bottom of the canvas was rising as they pulled it forward. Soon they would have to reach above their heads to keep hold of it – would they be able to pull it forward far enough?

To his surprise and concealed delight, Arthur had realised that the woman's words really did have no effect on him. Of course – it was not him she had primed to obey her orders in the cellar. It was Art, the *real* Art. But trapped at the point of

Macbeth's sword, he had little choice but to seem to obey.

He had been surprised and depressed when his words seemed to have no effect on the audience. He had heard Meg's shout that he needed to recite the whole speech and his heart fell. He had read the play – they had studied it at school. But could he recall the whole speech? He wasn't sure he even knew which appearance of the witches included the '*pricking of my thumbs*' bit. He tried desperately to think of words that might help.

The '*Double, double toil and trouble*' lines seemed to have an effect – he could hear the audience shuffle and stir. But now Macbeth was climbing up after him, and Eva Münster had started to climb the ladder at the other end of the gantry. Unless he could find out the words to recite, Arthur was trapped. He could not get past Eva in her rage, and he would not push an innocent actor possibly to his death . . .

'We need a copy of the script,' he yelled.

He could hear Jonny shouting something below, but could not make out the words. What was going on? He had seen a script somewhere, he remembered.

'Try the dressing rooms,' he shouted. Was there time? Where else could they find a script? He felt a surge of excitement as he realised. 'The prompter has a copy – the old lady by the side of the stage.'

'Not any more, she hasn't.' Eva had reached the gantry. She held up the copy of *Macbeth* that the prompter had been holding. 'You've given your farewell performance,' she hissed.

The gantry swayed as she stepped on to it. At the other end, Macbeth mirrored her action. Then he drew his sword and started towards Arthur.

'Jump!'

Arthur thought it was the woman, trying to order him again to kill himself.

'Art – it's your only chance. You have to jump!'

It was Meg's voice, coming from the stage below. Arthur looked down, saw Jonny and Meg waiting below. He gulped, ran towards Macbeth, then, as it seemed as if he must impale himself on the man's outstretched sword, over thirty feet above the stage, he leaped into space.

*

Hiding in the shadows at the bottom of the orchestra pit, Flinch heard Art's shouts. She had seen Jonny go speeding past and leap on to the stage, Meg close behind. They would save Art, she was sure. Which meant it was up to her to find the play.

There was a door at the back of the pit which gave out into a narrow passageway. Flinch ran along it and emerged – as she had hoped and guessed she would – into the dressing-room corridor. This was where Art had said she could find a copy of the play.

But what would it look like? Was it a book or a pile of papers? Big or small? She opened the first door she came to and looked round. Nothing, nothing that could possibly be it – no books or papers at all, just make-up and props.

The next room was the same.

But in the third she found a bundle of paper held together by string that was tied in a loop through a hole punched in the top left corner of the sheets. There was writing printed on the paper – a title on the cover. Flinch stared at it. Did it say *Macbeth*? She knew how to spell her own name, but little more. Should she keep looking, or take a chance that this was what Art needed?

Arthur hit the canvas, felt it give, thought he would tear a hole right through it and fall. Then he bounced, slid, gathered speed. It was like a fairground ride, like the giant inflatable slide they had at the park in the summer. He bounced again, tumbled on to his stomach, twisted round – the wind rushing past, paint flaking away under his hands as he tried to slow himself down. His palms were rubbed raw by the rough material. He could feel the heat through his trousers.

Then, suddenly, the canvas beneath him was gone and he was flying through the air. The orchestra pit opened up beneath him, but he cleared it, tumbling head over heels. He slammed into the fifth row of the audience, felt the air leave his lungs, and gasped and choked for breath as he sagged and fell.

A woman's hat went spinning away. She gasped and choked with Arthur as she scrabbled for breath. The man beside her was doubled up with the shock and the pain. But they said nothing. He hoped they had felt nothing.

Arthur himself felt winded and shocked and bruised and terrified. But he had escaped. He staggered to the end of the row, tripping and stumbling over the legs of the people sitting immobile and unseeing. He collapsed with relief into the narrow aisle at the side of the auditorium. There was a door close by, opposite the row in front of him – he could get backstage and hunt for a copy of the play.

As he dragged himself to his feet, the door swung open. Arthur felt almost sick as a cackle of inhuman laughter announced the arrival of the three witches. With a sob of pain and frustration, he turned and ran towards the back of the theatre. The witches hurried after him, screeching and shrieking with delight.

'Art!'

He looked across and saw Flinch keeping pace with him in the main aisle in the centre of the theatre. She was waving a bundle of papers.

'I got it, Art. I got it!' she cried excitedly.

A glance back at the stage told Arthur that Eva Münster was still watching them from the gantry, screaming and shouting at the witches to hurry, to catch them. He increased his speed, wishing he was as fast as Jonny. But he was leaving the witches behind as he turned and ran across the back of the theatre to join Flinch.

They almost collided, Arthur grabbing the playscript like a relay runner grabbing the baton. Together they continued running, while he leafed quickly through. Yes – it was the script for *Macbeth*. He recognised names and speeches. The text blurred and jumped and shimmered as he ran. But the play seemed too short.

Then he realised why. It was not the whole play. Just the pages for one actor – just his part. And he could see now that Malcolm's speeches were underlined. And he knew that Malcolm never met the witches, was never tainted by the world of the supernatural. Would be of no use.

'Is it the right papers?' Flinch gasped, and all Arthur could do was shake his head sadly.

They stopped to regain their breath. The witches too seemed to have stopped, perhaps they were exhausted as well.

'Fotherington!'

Eva's voice cut through the theatre like a dagger. Arthur and Flinch were at the back of the auditorium, diagonally opposite where Charlie was sitting with Sir Carmichael in the box at the front. They both saw Charlie slowly get to his feet, waiting for his instructions.

'The men at the back of the box,' Eva Münster shouted to him. 'They will be armed.'

She leaned forward, staring down at Arthur, though he doubted she could see him properly with the stage lights on. 'You think you have won,' she screeched. 'But you are too late. Even with the script and the words, you are too late. I can still win.'

Arthur watched Charlie walk slowly to the back of the box, where two men were standing either side of the door. He saw Charlie reach inside one of the men's jackets and take out a large revolver.

'Fotherington,' the woman was shouting again, 'take the gun.'

'No, Charlie, don't do it.'

Meg's voice was shrill and faint by comparison to Eva's. Charlie seemed not to hear.

'If I cannot control him for the Reich, then I shall kill him. Take the gun,' she screamed again, but there was triumph as well as desperation in her voice now. 'And shoot the Prime Minister.'

In slow motion, as if moving through water, Charlie raised the revolver. He pointed it directly at the head of the man sitting next to Sir Carmichael.

'Do it now – kill him!'

Flinch had not recognised the Prime Minister. Art had once met Mr Baldwin, she knew, but she, Meg and Jonny had not. He looked such an ordinary man, she thought – a bit short, smartly dressed, with an experienced, well-worn face, thinning dark hair and bushy eyebrows.

He sat impassively as Charlie aimed the gun at his head. Neither Arthur nor Flinch moved either. Time seemed to have stopped, framing the moment.

It started again with a sudden blur of motion. Jonny flew through the air, over the low wall round the box where the Prime Minister was sitting. He hammered into Charlie, sending him staggering just as the gun went off. The bullet cracked into the high ceiling of the theatre. Then Jonny was rolling and tumbling and trying to get up again.

Charlie seemed to recover first. He turned

slowly back towards the Prime Minister, who seemed not to have noticed what was happening around him. Again Charlie aimed the gun.

Arthur was running now, and so, Flinch realised with surprise, was she. Jonny's leap had shocked them back into life and they charged towards the front of the theatre. But before they had gone ten paces, the witches appeared in front of them. They held their hands up in front of their faces, their fingernails like tiny daggers.

Between the hissing figures, Flinch could see Jonny again charging at Charlie. Another sudden movement as Meg leaped over the side of the box and joined him. Together they struggled to pull Charlie away, to grab the gun, to wrestle it away from their friend.

Eva Münster was running back along the gantry, towards the ladder. She was shouting again. Though Flinch could barely hear her, she did not have to wonder what she was saying. Her instructions were obvious – the audience was getting to its feet. Heads were turning, people were moving. In a slow, shambling, funereal march, people shuffled along the rows and into the aisle. They turned and headed blank-faced towards the back of the theatre – towards Arthur and Flinch.

There was no way that they could hold Charlie for long, Meg realised. He seemed to have incredible strength, bringing the gun round again. Jonny was struggling to keep out of its way – they both knew that in his current controlled state, Charlie would shoot them to get at the Prime Minister and carry out his instructions.

But now danger was coming from another source. The two men at the back of the theatre box blinked as if waking from a dream and stepped forward. In unison they reached inside their jackets. One man took his hand out again, empty – Charlie already had his gun. The other drew a revolver.

'We can't stop them both,' Meg shouted.

It was worse than that, she realised. Sir Carmichael was turning in his seat, his hands reaching out for the Prime Minister's throat. In the main theatre the whole audience was slowly making its way towards where Arthur and Flinch were standing near the back.

'Forget Charlie,' Jonny shouted. With an almighty heave he sent the old man spinning away from them. He grabbed Meg's hand and dragged her across the box. As they went, he lowered his shoulder and barged the man with the gun out of the way. 'We have to get the Prime Minister!'

He was right, she realised. They could not stop the whole audience if the woman sent them to kill the Prime Minister, but they could perhaps – just perhaps – get the man to safety. Somehow. Somewhere.

Together they dragged Mr Baldwin from his seat. He was a stocky man and very heavy – a dead weight as he made no effort to help them. Somehow they managed it, just for a moment. But as they started to drag him towards the door at the back of the box, Sir Carmichael's hands closing where his throat had been, the Prime Minister fell. It was as if his legs didn't know how to support him. They buckled and he slipped from Meg and Jonny's grip.

As he fell, a shot cracked out – the bullet whining through the air above the falling Prime Minister. If they had managed to keep him upright, Meg realised, he would be dead.

Charlie and the man with the gun were stepping slowly towards them. Their faces, expressions, even their eyes were completely blank. Jonny put his head down and charged at them full speed. The two men were thrown backwards and Jonny collapsed as well, winded. But the men immediately started to rise again.

In their efforts to get up, neither of them paid any attention to Jonny. Their staring eyes remained fixed on the Prime Minister and Meg. She watched, holding her breath, as Jonny seemed to recover, reached up, wrenched the gun from the Prime Minister's bodyguard. He flung it as hard as he could from the box and it skidded across the stage, out of sight. Out of reach. Jonny was going for Charlie's gun now, but the bodyguard pushed him aside.

Meg looked down at the prone body of Stanley Baldwin. She could never lift him on her own. She doubted she could drag him far. Sir Carmichael got stiffly to his feet and turned towards Meg. He took a step forwards. Meg thought he was going to fall – his foot slipped on something and he lurched sideways. But he regained his balance and took another step.

Instinctively, Meg glanced down to see what the man had slipped on. It was a book. She could recall it falling from the Prime Minister's lap as they lifted him up, though she had not paid it any attention.

She did now.

It was a copy of *Macbeth*.

Following Jonny's example, Meg put her head down and ran. She managed to knock Sir Carmichael sideways. He staggered back, crashing into Charlie, and they both fell in a tangle of arms and legs. Charlie's gun clattered to the floor. Behind them the disarmed bodyguard waited patiently for them to rise.

On the floor where she had fallen, Meg scooped up the book. It was a slim volume with a plain hard cover. 'Jonny!' she screamed as loudly as she could, flinging the book across the box to where she had last seen him.

It spun between the rising figures of Charlie and Sir Carmichael. It just missed the bodyguard's shoulder. Rising to his feet behind them, Jonny had to leap to catch the book. He fumbled it, almost dropped it, clasped it tight to his chest.

'Find the right passage in the play,' Meg shouted. 'Read the words!'

But Jonny didn't even open the book.

*

He knew he could never find the right part of the play. He had no idea where to start or really what he was looking for. But Art would know.

A glance was enough to tell Jonny that he could not get to Art through the auditorium. It was packed with people pushing their way out of the rows of seats and processing towards the rear of the theatre, where Flinch and Art were backing away. No way through, and too far to throw the book like Meg had done.

Charlie was on his feet again, stooping to retrieve the gun he had dropped. He had seconds at the most, Jonny realised.

He ran.

The bodyguard at the back of the box stepped across in front of the door, but Jonny was not to be stopped now. He elbowed the man aside almost without slowing and wrenched the door open. Then he was running full tilt along the narrow passage down the side of the theatre. It must lead to the foyer, he reasoned. If not, then all was lost.

It seemed to take for ever before he emerged into the foyer. Immediately Jonny skidded, spun, felt his feet slipping on the stone floor as he changed direction, then they got a purchase and propelled him forward again. Into the back of the auditorium.

The people from the back rows of the audience were between him and Art now. He could see Art's head through the crowd. Could see Art looking round desperately for a way of escape.

'Art!' he screamed. Jonny hoped he could hear, hoped he would realise what was happening. Jonny flung the book.

Jonny would be too late, Meg could see that. She stepped over the prone body of the Prime Minister and, as Charlie took aim one last time, she stood between them. In front of the gun.

She heard Jonny's shout from the back of the theatre, dared to turn to watch, saw the book spin through the air towards where Art was standing. She saw Art jump, reach, almost catch the book. She saw him miss. The book fell into the crowd of people behind him. Out of reach.

Arthur felt physically sick as he saw the book fall. His fingers had brushed the cover as it sailed past.

He *should* have caught in. But it was too late now. He saw it fall into the group of people in front of him. They had their arms outstretched like sleepwalkers – like zombies from a late-night horror film. Stepping slowly forwards as they reached out for Arthur's throat. The book was trampled and ignored under their feet.

He looked round for Flinch, wondering how he could comfort her now. Wondering if she knew she was about to die.

Flinch had gone.

Without hesitation or thought, as soon as she saw Art had missed the book, as soon as she saw it fall into the crowd, Flinch hurled herself forwards. She dived at the feet of the approaching people, managed to scrabble between their legs. She was trapped in a moving forest of human trees, scrabbling to get through, clutching at people as she pulled herself forwards, her eyes focused on glimpses of the book as the people moved round her.

She squeezed and wriggled and shoved. She hammered at legs in her way, fought round people, felt feet kicking at her, stepping on her.

She turned quickly away as a boot came down almost on her face, a ragged end of bootlace whipping at her cheek. Arms outstretched, she clawed her way forwards until she could reach the book.

Arthur gave a startled cry as he saw Flinch suddenly leap up in the middle of the approaching crowd. He had no time to remain surprised, though, as the book was again flying through the air towards him. This time, he thought, this time he *had* to catch it.

But it was too high. It would pass well above his head and to the side. Instead of jumping for the book, knowing he could not catch it, he threw himself sideways.

A hand grabbed at him and tried to pull him back. But Arthur managed to rip himself free. Still running, he stepped on to the arm of the chair at the end of the row, next step was the back of the seat, then he was flying into the air as he propelled himself upwards.

The very tips of his outstretched fingers knocked into the book as it flew past, knocking it upwards. It dipped and fell as Arthur too fell back.

He landed on his feet, staggered, caught his balance. And the book fell into his outstretched hands.

At once he had it open, flicking through the pages. Where was that scene? Where? The print was a blur. But by some miracle of chance, he saw the words, caught the pages as they riffled past, turned back. How much did he have to recite? How much time did he have? Arthur shouted out the text at the top of his voice as the hands grabbed at him and dragged him down.

'Double, double toil and trouble.'

Meg heard Art's voice muffled but audible above the hubbub around her.

'Fire burn, and cauldron bubble.'

Charlie had the gun still aimed, as if Meg were not there – was he going to shoot through her, she wondered? She had her answer as Sir Carmichael's hands closed on her shoulders and dragged her away.

'Cool it with a baboon's blood . . .'

Charlie stepped forward, standing over the Prime Minister, the gun pointed straight down at the man's head. Behind him, Meg could see Eva

Münster running across the stage towards the box. Her face was a mask of rage and she was screaming incoherently. She was holding the gun that Jonny had flung across the stage.

'*Then the charm is firm and good.*'

Charlie's head seemed to sag. The revolver slipped from his fingers and dropped to the floor, just missing the Prime Minister's head.

'*By the pricking of my thumbs,*'

Art's voice seemed louder and clearer now. Meg realised this was because everyone had stopped. People were frozen in mid-step, arms outstretched. Even Eva Münster had stopped. Her face was white, her red lips quivering, her eyes wide. The gun trembling in her hand.

'*Something wicked this way comes.*'

Charlie seemed to wake. His head snapped up, and he gave a gasp of astonishment as he saw Mr Baldwin lying at his feet, a gun on the floor beside him. The Prime Minister too seemed to be waking, groaning and stretching and getting slowly to his feet. The audience was milling about in confusion, muttering at first but then talking more loudly.

On the stage, Eva Münster was again

intoning the words of *Macbeth*. Her blood red lips moved furiously as she primed yet another mind – her own. In one hand she held the stone aloft. With the other hand, she raised the gun.

And fired.

At the same moment, the curtain dropped rapidly, closing the performance. Cutting off Meg's view of the woman's body sprawled across the stage.

With no control at all over his own body, Art climbed the ladder – hand over hand, step by step. The stage receded below. Sarah and the witches stood in a group, watching. They made no attempt to follow him. Did they know what was happening? Or was it simply because they knew there was nowhere for Art to go when he got to the top. He could walk out along the narrow metal gantry but that was it. There was a ladder down from the other end to the far side of the stage. But if he climbed down again they would be waiting for him. Not that he had any choice in the matter.

The one thing he had achieved, Art realised, was that the witches had stopped their chanting. But even as he thought this, Sarah whirled round far below him and waved the witches back to their cauldron with a snarl of anger.

'*Gall of goat and slips of yew,*' they chanted, whirling once more round the stage. '*Silver'd in the moon's eclipse . . .*'

He was at the top of the ladder now, hoping desperately that he would stop, or regain some control of his own movement. Art was not scared of heights, but the glimpses he got of the stage far below made him giddy. He stepped out on to the gantry and walked slowly, cautiously forward. He hoped he retained his sense of balance.

'*Nose of Turk and Tartar's lips . . .*'

He had to pick his way carefully along the metal walkway. Lights were attached to it at intervals – shining down at the stage, but mounted in brackets on the gantry. He could feel the heat from them as he passed. The enormous mound of brushwood reached up almost to the level of the gantry. He could not focus on the whole length of the pile at once, so looking down along it made the ground seem even further away.

Art stopped, turned sideways. His toes were over the edge of the narrow walkway. In a sudden flash of numbing fear, he knew what he was going to do. And that there was no way he could stop himself. As if someone else was controlling his actions and had determined that this was his fate. The ground blurred and swam far below as the witches spun and chanted . . .

'*Double, double toil and trouble; fire burn, and cauldron bubble.*'

And high above the stage, Art leaped forward off the gantry. Into space.

It was as if his own control of his body had been switched back on. As soon as he leaped, Art regained his power of movement. But he was already flying off the gantry, his arms flailing uselessly.

One hand slapped against the hot casing of a huge lamp projecting from the gantry. He grabbed it desperately, tried to wrap his other hand round it. Struggled to hold on.

But the metal was scorching hot and his cry turned into a shriek of pain. His weight was tearing the lamp from its bracket, wrenching it free. His feet kicked out with the continuing momentum of his fall, swung sideways, caught another lamp. It was smaller, a spotlight, and his kick sent it flying. The electrical cable snaked out behind it as it fell.

The best Art could do was swing himself sideways before the pain and the fact that the light was also falling forced him to let go. But it was enough.

Rather than falling towards the stage, he crashed into the pile of brushwood. His weight carried him through it, breaking and snapping the dry branches and twigs. He closed his eyes tight, hands over his head as the broken wood scratched and tore at his face. He could feel it digging into his flesh and catching in his clothes. His whole body was being stabbed with sharp sticks as he continued to fall. But he was slowing, slowing. Until eventually he was held immobile in the middle of the shattered pyramid of wood.

He opened his eyes, and saw Sarah's face contorted with a mixture of anger and triumph as she stared into the tangle of broken branches.

'*Cool it with a baboon's blood,*' keened the witches. '*Then the charm is firm and good.*'

The huge arc light smashed down into the

wood beside Art, trailing its cable. The bulb exploded in a shower of sparks as the end of a branch went through it. The light stopped close beside Art, cable stretched to breaking point, sparks spitting towards him. One of them landed on his cheek, making him cry out, then shake it free. Others rained down close beside him as he struggled to get out of the pile of broken wood. But wherever he tried to put his weight, the wood broke away beneath him. It was like thrashing in water or quicksand as he tried to gain a purchase.

There was a smell of burning, he realised. At first he thought it was where the spark had whipped at his cheek. Then he saw that the light was still sparking and spluttering, and the wood beside it was crackling as tiny red and yellow flowers of flame blossomed. Trails of acrid smoke began pumping out from the wood, making him cough as he struggled to escape.

He tumbled to the floor, retching. The smoke was billowing round the theatre now as the woodpile caught like a bonfire. Tinder-dry and with the fire starting right in the middle of it, the wood was ablaze in no time.

The witches were coughing as the smoke tore

at their throats and they struggled to complete their lines.

'*By the pricking of my thumbs . . .*'

But they got no further.

Art staggered away from the fire and into a rainstorm. Sprinklers had cascaded into life all across the ceiling as soon as they detected the smoke. Cold and refreshing.

A shape loomed out of the foggy air in front of Art, resolving itself into Sarah. 'What have you done?' she screamed at Art. 'You will pay for this!'

Beside her, other shapes became solid. Three of the caryatids lurched forwards unsteadily. One of them, Art saw, was already on fire. The water from the sprinklers was struggling to quell the flames that danced on the creature's outstretched arm as she reached out towards Art. Without thinking, he lashed out with his foot and kicked it squarely in the chest – driving it back into the other two wooden figures.

The stage was slick with burning debris and water. The caryatid Art had kicked slipped and stumbled, dragging one of the other two down as it fell. The third swayed, then toppled after them like a skittle. In moments, despite the sprinklers, the fire had spread across the wood. Perhaps the polished finish of the figures was inflammable, Art thought as he stumbled past.

Sarah was standing with her arms outstretched, screaming.

'I am burning,' she shrieked as the fire spread round her.

Without thinking, Art grabbed her and dragged her with him to the edge of the stage. Over the edge. Falling.

There was less smoke down below the stage level. Looking back, Art saw a pillar of flame where the wood had been. Smoke was pumping out of it. The lights up on the gantry exploded one after another as they overheated, showering down sparks. He pulled Sarah to her feet. Her face was bleached white, her eyes open wide in horror and surprise.

'What's happening?' she gasped.

All around, people were rising to their feet as well.

'We have to get out of here,' Art shouted. 'Everyone out, quick!'

Even if anyone heard above the crackle of the flames and the confused gasps and shouts of the awakened audience, they did not need telling. The three witches leaped off the stage, leading the race for the exits. Dragging Sarah with him, Art ran. He pushed past anyone in his way, desperate to get back to the row where they had been sitting at the start of the performance.

Grandad was waiting at the end of the row. He took Art's hand and allowed himself to be pulled with Sarah towards the foyer.

CHAPTER FIFTEEN

Algernon Makepeace Gregson had woken up at the back of the theatre, perplexed to find the performance apparently over. His bemusement had been exceeded only by his embarrassed surprise at discovering that Arthur and the other children were actually friends of Sir Carmichael and Lord Fotherington.

Sir Carmichael had explained this in a few terse words, then sent Gregson to supervise the departure of the equally bemused audience. Gregson muttered under his breath as he left them with Sir Carmichael and Charlie in his office. But Arthur suspected he would soon get over the shock and relish the chance to ingratiate himself with such important people.

Now there was just Charlie, Sir Carmichael, Arthur, Meg, Jonny and Flinch in the office.

'No one in the audience seems to remember anything much,' Charlie said. 'Even the Prime Minister.'

'And what about you?' Meg said.

'Oh, I remember all right,' Charlie said.

'I know that something happened,' Sir Carmichael told them. 'But it's all a bit hazy. Like a dream. If no one had told me otherwise, I'd assume I'd watched the play and perhaps dozed off for a bit in the middle. I can remember the performance.'

'The performance that never took place,' Jonny said. 'How come you remember what happened, Charlie?'

'I'm not sure,' he confessed. 'It was very strange. As Sir Carmichael said, it was like a dream, I knew what was going on and what I was doing, only I couldn't help it. I kept willing myself to wake up.'

'Perhaps because you had been hypnotised before,' Arthur suggested. 'Down in the cellar, where the magician keeps his things.'

Despite it all being over, Arthur was feeling despondent. He had hoped, expected even, that once everything was sorted out and everyone else was back to normal again, he would be back in his own time – would have swapped back with the real Art. The way he had been transported back must be to do with the strange stone and Eva's attempts at mind control. But she was dead now, and he was still here. He was beginning to think he might be stuck back in the 1930s for ever. He looked round at his new friends. Perhaps, he thought, that wouldn't be so bad. But it was still a huge wrench, and he would miss Sarah . . . How much should he tell the others? When should he tell them? What should he tell them? How would he cope, playing Brandon Lake?

Flinch was standing by the open door, leaning against the wall and looking bored. Arthur caught her eye and she smiled.

'What happened to that horrible woman?' Meg was asking.

'Now that is odd,' Charlie said. 'It obviously wasn't a priority to check on her, apart from making sure she was no longer a danger. So we left her where she was while we made sure the Prime Minister was safe and got him away.'

'Then we had to check the people in the audience had no idea what had happened,' Sir Carmichael added. 'Tricky,' he went on with a smile, 'given that I didn't know either, or the Prime Minister's people. No one apart from you and Charlie knows anything for certain, it seems.'

'But she is dead?' Arthur said, suddenly

feeling cold at the thought she might have survived and escaped.

'Oh, yes,' Charlie assured them. 'She is quite, quite dead. I could tell that at once.'

'She shot herself,' Meg said. 'I saw, as the curtain dropped. She was chanting something, and raised the gun. Then I heard the shot. I saw her fall.'

'She fired a shot, certainly,' Charlie agreed. 'But in fact it barely grazed her skull. That isn't what killed her.'

'Then what did?' Jonny asked in surprise.

'I have no idea,' Charlie told them. 'Neither has the doctor. Completely baffled.'

'Heart failure, he says,' Sir Carmichael said. 'Which means it could be anything.'

Charlie was holding something up. 'This was clenched in her hand. She wasn't about to let it go, I can tell you. Though I have no idea what it is.'

Jonny knew, as did they all. 'It's Mr Jerrickson's stone,' he said at once.

'Mr Jerrickson's?' Charlie was surprised.

'We'll see he gets it back,' Meg said, and Charlie shrugged and handed it to her.

Sir Carmichael put his hand to his head.

'Gets more curious by the minute,' he said. 'Though I can't say all this excitement has done much for my own injury, but at least I'm still here.'

'It hasn't helped us find the theatre ghost either,' Meg said.

'Oh, I have an idea about that,' Arthur said, forcing a smile.

He looked round at their expectant faces. But when he looked towards the door he saw that Flinch had gone.

He had no time to wonder at this. They all heard it – a whispering hiss that seemed suddenly to fill the room. The words were indistinct – 'ooh' and 'ah' and other almost soothing sounds. But the way they echoed quietly in the room was far from soothing.

'The ghost!' Jonny gasped, his face white.

'Where's Flinch?' Meg said as she too realised the girl had gone. 'It's taken Flinch!'

'It hasn't taken Flinch,' Arthur reassured them. 'And I think I know where the ghost is.'

'You want to go and catch it?' Jonny asked, appalled.

*

The steps down to the cellar were shrouded in shadows. Light seemed to disappear into the gloom as Arthur led Jonny and Meg into the blackness. He could hear Charlie and Sir Carmichael behind them, but he did not look back. As his eyes became more accustomed to the darkness, he could see that there was some light ahead – the flickering of a candle.

The ghostly voice was getting louder as they went deeper. It echoed round the stone walls – a medley of noises that somehow failed to quite resolve themselves into real words. Just incoherent sounds. But Arthur knew what they were now, and he was not afraid.

They made their way towards the light. Arthur had his hand on the wall as he felt his way. If he concentrated, he thought he could see the vague shapes of his feet as he shuffled nervously along. The flickering light was getting brighter, coming from just around the end of the wall.

The wall ended. Arthur smiled and stepped out into the pale light. He glanced back, beckoning to Meg and Jonny to join him, knowing they could now see him illuminated in the candlelight.

The sounds stopped, and the ghostly voice said, 'Oh, hello.'

As Arthur had guessed, it was Flinch. She was sitting cross-legged on the cold stone floor, a lighted candle close beside her.

'There's no lights, but I found the candle and some matches,' she said.

She raised her hands, and they could see that she was holding a white rabbit. She held it close to her face, and cooed at it gently, reassuringly. She ooh-ed and ah-ed, and Jonny's nervous expression became a grin as he realised that this was the sound they had heard, only echoed and distorted.

'You're the ghost, Flinch,' Meg told her.

Flinch put down the rabbit and stared at them wide-eyed. 'I am?'

'It seems so,' said Sir Carmichael, joining them. 'The sound from this cellar carries, probably along the pipes. You can hear it in the corridor above and some of the storerooms.'

'But Flinch wasn't the ghost before,' Jonny said. 'So who was?'

'Eva Münster,' Arthur explained. It all seemed so obvious now – obvious and slightly mundane. 'The ghostly voice was reciting bits of *Macbeth*. The scene with the witches, like I read to break the spell.'

'She was rehearsing,' Meg realised. 'Practising, or actually hypnotising people.'

Arthur nodded. 'Without realising she could be heard.'

'You said about the cellar,' Flinch said, 'and I remembered the magician said his things were down here. And he never came back, so I thought they must still be here. And I remembered his rabbit, and I thought it must be down here on its own.' She picked up the rabbit again, looking closely into its face. It wrinkled its nose at her happily. 'I think he's hungry,' she said.

Jonny heaved a huge sigh of relief. 'That's the second time you've spooked us, Flinch,' he said. 'I hope it's the last, don't you, Art?'

But Arthur barely heard him. He staggered as if he had been hit. The world seemed to somersault over him and Jonny's voice faded until it was gone. The flickering candlelight was fading too – disappearing down the wrong end of a telescope. Vanishing into infinity.

*

'What is it? Are you all right?' Jonny was saying.

Meg grabbed at Art's shoulders, holding him upright.

Art blinked, trying to clear his blurred vision. He felt weak at the knees, and he was grateful for Meg's support. He sighed – a great long breath that echoed round the cellar. 'Sorry,' he said. 'Yes, I'm fine.' When he looked up, he had a huge smile on his face. 'I'm fine now,' he said. And he was – everything was somehow back to normal. He was again down in the cellar, and he was with his friends. 'Glad to be back,' he said.

'Back?' Jonny said. 'What are you talking about?'

'Well,' Charlie said, 'I think perhaps we should make our way upstairs. Bring your new friend, Flinch. We'll make sure he's fed and looked after and returned to his owner, won't we?'

'Indeed we shall,' Sir Carmichael confirmed. 'Oh, and here's something for you, Art. Souvenir.' He held something out. But in the dimness of the candlelight, Art could not see what it was.

Later that night, Art almost fell into bed he was so exhausted. But at least, he thought happily, it was his own bed in his own room – his own time. He had been trying to work out how it had happened. A coincidence, he decided – a combination of events. Eva Münster's attempts to control his mind, enhanced and focused by her use of the stone. The stone was the key – it was something that existed in both their times, Art's and Arthur's. They had both stared into it, perhaps both at the same moment, all those years apart, as the words from *Macbeth* were spoken to them. And somehow, in that split moment, their minds had become muddled. Just as now, they had been swapped back, as time papered over the cracks in reality.

Art was already almost asleep, but there was one thing he wanted to do before he finally closed his eyes for the night.

He took the casebook from the drawer by his bed and turned to his last entry. He was surprised to see that Arthur had added a few lines, and his fingers ran down the tear in the page where it looked as if the pen had slipped. He thought for a moment about taking out the page. But no – he would leave it. He could hardly write about his own experiences of the last few days, so he would leave Arthur's enigmatic entry there as a reminder instead.

There was a bottle of spirit gum in the drawer beside the book. Art took the souvenir that Sir Carmichael had given him and carefully gummed one top corner on the back of it. Then he glued it in the book under Arthur's words. That too would serve as a reminder – an invitation to a very special performance of *Macbeth*.

'I thought I would go back,' Art said. 'When all this was over, I thought I would go back ... home.'

Grandad, Sarah and Art were sitting on the pavement opposite the theatre. They had watched as the audience streamed out. They had watched Miles Kershaw and his camera team hurrying to get shots of the evacuation and stopping people for comments. They looked as stunned as everyone else. The flames licked up out of the roof of the theatre, and the first fire engines arrived in a screeching of sirens and flashing lights.

An hour later, the fire was all but out, though

the hoses were still pouring gallons of water into the building.

'It's a mercy no one was hurt,' Art heard one of the firemen say as he went past.

'It's the words, Shakespeare's lines, that somehow did it,' Grandad explained. 'Together with the stone that focuses the mind. The same lines being repeated in both times provided a link between the two times, just as the clock does.' He smiled. 'And perhaps there really is a little magic in Shakespeare's words. Who knows?'

'But can we get our Arthur back?' Sarah wondered. She still looked pale and shaken, though she insisted she was all right.

'Oh, I should think so,' Grandad said. He was smiling. 'The play's the thing, you know. We just need to complete the act.'

Art held up his hand. 'Before we do that, I want to be sure . . .' He turned to Sarah. Her face was smudged from the smoke, but she was managing a brave smile. 'Are you certain everything is all right?' he asked.

'I'm fine now. She's gone. There was a voice in my head at first. She was in control of me somehow. But when the fire started, and the theatre began to burn, she ... went.' Sarah shrugged, unable to explain more than that.

Grandad was nodding. 'I've had a long time to think about it, and I believe I know what happened. Eva Münster, when she was defeated in 1937, managed to put her mind, her very soul, into the fabric of the theatre itself – that was why and how it seemed to come to life. Her mind controlling it and struggling to be free. Just as she primed the people she hypnotised to perform a specific task when they heard the words of *Macbeth*, so she trained her own mind to reawaken and, it seems, seek out a suitable new body.'

'Thanks,' Sarah said.

'They say,' Grandad told them, 'that Shakespeare drew on real spells and black magic when he wrote *Macbeth*. That's why there's so much superstition about performing or even quoting it.' He paused as several firemen ran by, dragging a hose. 'There will be rather more now, I fancy,' he added. 'Right, young man, are you ready?'

Art took a deep breath and nodded.

'And do you have the stone? To focus on?'

Taking the stone from his pocket, he smiled at Grandad, squeezed Sarah's hand. 'Goodbye,' he said.

'I hope,' he added, with a thin smile. Then he looked down into the depths of the stone cradled in his hand. Watched the swirling depths of colour dancing like flames inside.

'*By the pricking of my thumbs,*' Grandad said quietly, '*something wicked this way comes . . .*'

Nothing happened. So far as Sarah could tell, there was no change. Slowly, hesitantly, nervously, Arthur looked up from the stone in his hand.

'Did it work?' she asked, her voice hoarse and raw from the smoke of the fire.

'Of course it worked,' Grandad said. 'Didn't it?'

'Yes,' Arthur said, and the relief was evident in his voice. 'Yes, it worked.'

'Then it's over.' Sarah laughed out loud with relief. She leaned forward and grabbed Arthur, pulling him into a hug.

For a moment, he let her hold him. Then he pulled away. 'No,' he said. 'It's not over yet. Not quite.'

Grandad was holding something out to him. 'Will this do?'

Sarah saw that it was a lump of stone, the

edges ragged and broken. Left over from the restoration work on the theatre, she assumed.

Art took it and weighed it in his hand. He nodded. Then, without comment, he placed the strange pebble he had been holding on the pavement between them. It seemed to catch and reflect the light, glowing with swirling fiery colour. Sarah found herself drawn to look at it, unable to turn away, her mind slowly filling with the kaleidoscopic pattern.

Then Art brought the lump of stone down heavily, breaking the spell, freeing her mind. Shattering the glowing pebble into sharp, sparkling fragments. Again and again he smashed the stone into the fragments, until all that was left was a fine, white powder.

'Wherever she is,' he said quietly, 'she can't come back.'

Sarah took Arthur's hand. Grandad was nodding slowly in agreement.

'It's over now,' Arthur said.